W9-AUY-031

Logic

ALSO BY OLYMPIA VERNON

Eden

OLYMPIA VERNON

LOGIC

Grove Press
New York

Published simultaneously in Canada
Printed in the United States of America

FIRST EDITION

Library of Congress Cataloging-in-Publication Data
Vernon, Olympia.
Logic / Olympia Vernon.—1st ed.
p. cm.
ISBN 0-8021-1771-6
1. African American teenage girls—Fiction.   2. Alienation
(Social psychology)—Fiction.   3. African American families—Fiction.
4. Teenage girls—Fiction.   5. Mississippi—Fiction.   6. Scandals—
Fiction.   7. Aunts—Fiction.   I. Title.
PS3622.E75L64 2004
813'.6—dc22   2003067524

Grove Press
841 Broadway
New York, NY 10003

04 05 06 07 08   10 9 8 7 6 5 4 3 2 1

To God, the angels, John Coumes, Matt Clark,
and Terry Traylor

"Go outside, laugh, and take a breath of
fresh air," a voice cries within me.
—Anne Frank: *The Diary of a Young Girl*

LOGIC

prologue

The lamb is called for.

And is struck a heavy blow.

It stumbles for a moment: the head open, the mouth vertical. Were it able to lift the hairs of its head, perhaps, it could have stopped the blood from coming down.

It cannot.

The eye moves.

The lid, as if controlled by voice and voice alone, hears the sound of a man calling another, a long word; a long death breathes nakedly behind the blood where the red is turning sharp.

The red is a verb.

The red is a shout.

There, vibrating behind the lobe, is the sound of His footsteps, the feeling of His hands lifting the creature onto His lap and sewing its head back together.

And when done, He evaporates: His arm slightly lifted above the hip bone, or where it would rest were He human, not in an effort to intimidate but to cause the red to breathe again.

For He was that He is.

And He could hear the blood of the lamb shouting.

He had already happened and was happening again.

chapter
one

David Harris was loading his pistol when the sun began to burn.

He paused for a moment, the light coming toward him. My God, he could have run right now and caught it, his hands and body and full self trapped by it. But he knew, down there where words turn to jelly, that he had nowhere to put it.

Just then he heard his daughter, Logic, ask Too how to spell *heaven*.

He looked at his wife, Too, how molecular she was. Too was a maid and midwife for the folks in Valsin County, Mississippi. Everything that went into her mouth was broken into tiny pieces— the bones in her face fragile, the empty breasts, as if there was no fat beneath her nipples to push her self-esteem forward. Open your mouth and record the distance between air and lung, and you will notice an invisible line wrapped so tightly around the bones in Too Harris's throat that the transparency of the distance itself will cause you to suffocate.

She took the cast-iron skillet off the fire and turned away from the stove, the sound of birds trampling on a large oak tree, and faced her daughter, the child she had named Logic, because she had seen the word on one of the Missis' magazines: a pale woman on the cover, her face upright and crooked, as if someone had dropped her entire body on concrete and cracked it at the jawbone.

Finally, she answered Logic's question. "I s'pose you spell something like that by lookin' up," she said. And then, as if confirming the space of thought in her head, she repeated, "Yeah, you spell *heaven* by lookin' up."

Logic's father, David, had loaded the pistol.

He laid the gun down on the table beside her. Now he was thinking of the manner in which he entered the world. He could almost remember sound, its first coming, instinctual, a finger going down his throat, forcing him to cry.

He felt the finger again, on his palate, as the voice of a man fell down upon his ears and made him cry even louder this time, the sound of a boy losing his strength.

He picked up the gun and looked out into the heat: the wooden boards of the house were rotting from the inside. He had built this triangular house with what was left of his hands; he was sort of a mathematician. He had set each board perfectly into the map of the house, except one that lay unevenly on the rooftop; he had found it on the side of the road. A metal loop had been hammered into it, a chain looped through the center. Steel.

"Where you headed?" The voice of his wife, Too, caused a gap in his breathing.

"Nowhere," he said.

With this, he opened the door to the house he had built with his own hands—to prove to himself that he was not completely a wasted mold of clay. He whispered something, his hand up to his mouth for a moment, as if he had been working on something combustible and it exploded in his face.

* * *

Logic was in her bedroom lying on her back. She had long since touched her belly and discovered a cloud of butterflies floating around inside.

She could feel them again.

She began to laugh. She solved almost everything this way, with laughter. She felt a wing fluttering in her ovary. She touched her abdomen and began to follow the rhythm of blood flowing there. Or something else.

Her room was the coldest. Even in summer, a breeze rode the space of her intimate bedroom, as she opened her mouth and caught it.

She had not completely healed from the accident. Her mother came home from work one day and found her lying in the dust; she had fallen from the oak tree, her head filled with blood. Too thought she had been struck by a metal rod or an animal and washed the redness from her head; when Logic came to, she said she had fallen from the sky.

Too gave her an elixir and waited for her to fall asleep.

Something was there in the room. She heard it breathing and could almost see the thing she had heard pick up the square-shaped pillow with both hands, stand there above Logic's head, and come down upon it. There was a terrible gasp. You must bear down, kill the girl before she gasps again. In a little while she will be dead, and Too Harris will be in a white woman's window, watching the energy of a moving cloud. What had she done?

Then, as if impossible, Too Harris realized that she alone was in the room.

And she alone was holding the pillow.

She hurried, as if urgency would cause her to forget, and collected a sewing needle, returning to Logic's bedside, where she had set the tools of surgery on an alabaster-white cloth: fishing twine, alcohol, fresh cotton, a leech.

Logic was fast asleep when Too picked up the parasite and watched as it sucked the poison out of her child's head. She soaked the cotton with alcohol and pressed down on the cut. Next, the threading of the needle. The fishing twine entered the needle's eye; she lifted the soft flesh of Logic's scalp. The wound began to rise.

She had closed it up.

A few days later, she noticed that the child who had come from her stomach was no longer balanced in her footsteps. Part of her body seemed to have been metallicized. When she found her, she was in the shape of 45 degrees. Her words were not the same; they did not come from her body in the pattern of stars: every syllable surrounding her attitude, attached like a vein, a molecule.

But for her laughter, Logic had become invisible.

The butterflies had stopped their fluttering. Logic lifted herself from the bed. She looked around at the life-sized doll in the corner of the room. Of all the things around her—the lime-colored dinosaur with a horizontal bar of pink tape over its mouth; the musical clef note that she had traced from a tombstone; a paring knife, its sharp edge stained with blue ink, violated. But the doll—the doll she loved—the only thing given to her by her father after she had fallen from the sky.

She called it Celesta.

Her mother was in the next room. The house was built this way: three rooms on one side, the third being the operating room, where she had lain, after being sewn back together, on a long steel table her father had bought from a man in Pyke County. The man was convinced he had seen the feet of Jesus in the center of it and could not keep it because he was a sinner and did not want God in his house: he was plastic.

"Logic!" yelled Too. "You best be gettin' to bed now."

The doll was in Logic's hands. She looked at the face where she had painted her lips candy-apple red, the dark pupils she had slowly begun to gouge out because they were artificial, the almond-colored skin. "I know."

Soon after, she began to undress. She looked at herself in the mirror—her breasts were beginning to swell. Her body was emaciated; she felt she had a pyramid in her bones. The straight, invisible line that connected her nipples, the perfect navel in the center of her stomach, creating the image of a measurement that was equal on all sides—she had inherited the genes of her father the mathematician.

She parted the hairs on her head and touched the feeling. Yes, it was the parasite that had left its feeling upon her. She felt it tickling her at times: the blood racing, pounding upward. She could control the feeling when she wanted.

By swallowing.

There on the edge of her dresser lay the panties and gown that her mother had readied for her. She was thirteen now, but she had not learned the stability of time, how things were to be put in order. She lived in a place where time did not exist; she dreamed, on many occasions, of death and believed it came in threes. This is the memory that lived within her: three spirits into the Ultimate one, the number of days at a time that she'd stopped eating, the pointed invisible lines of the triangle, the alphabets of YOU— those which she added to herself, her vocabulary with a distinction that required no urgency, as it passed through her lungs—a slow rising of the tongue, as if a baby had slept there unmoved.

She knelt down, her hands folded, and began to talk to God.

Her mother lay on the other side of the wall, her flat body against the sheets. Her room was without light. She turned to ask

God something and grew faceless, as if she did not exist at all in this unbehaved environment, as if it were God in the room with her in the early day, watching her hold the pillow: He saw she had suffocated the child, if only in her dreams.

For a spell, that season which comes and goes when a woman is restless, fascinated by her own accident, she wanted to crawl into bed with her daughter, ask her to pray for the thing that held the moment in its hands, so it would not come back again. Perhaps she knew that, were it to return, there would be a gasp that would split the belly of a quiet cloud and land high, up there where things go noticed, and come down, like oxygen, upon the earth and crush it.

Logic blew out the flame of a small lantern that stood beside her bed. The scent of the kerosene rose in the air, as she imagined herself opening up from the inside, where she believed there was a bed of larvae. Soon she would need an open door, a valve, to release them into the earth again. The image lay bound to the ink of the paring knife—its wings soon to be carved on the surface of her stomach.

When her father came home, his feet winding down, stopping near the operating room, she turned over and reminded herself to staple Celesta's lips together by morning.

chapter
two

The sun had risen into an unkept alphabet, the rim burning.

Logic was on the front porch laying her head down on some-thing cold when she saw George's children across the road, the faces smeared as if made of henna. Or ash. There were four in all. One girl and three boys, one of them fresh from the tubes; Too had pulled each of them out, headfirst. The others had evaporated in blood.

Only one of them mattered to Logic, he whom she called the tallest. He had reminded her of something scientific: perhaps the elephant he closely resembled, the bone of his forehead swollen and loose, as if he searched for a ladle to lay the bone down. Or the vowel he had come to be in her life, dangling from the limb of a high branch, its legs, its body aware of its power. And there too, beside him, was curtis, closest in age to the newborn baby.

curtis was as invisible to her as the butterflies in her stomach. She knew she was of no importance to him; he still memorized things in squares.

So was George's daughter; she was invisible.

She could not forget the baby, the morning the tallest ran for Too to pull him out of George's stomach—how George was as stiff as a block of ice, her hands and feet frozen, turned downward, epileptic. Her hair was wet and coarse; the baby had taken all her strength. How she lay there out in the open, her down-below exposed.

How the baby cried in the arms of the old woman! No one knew what the old woman meant to George, but she had sat there after the baby came out, rocking him to sleep on the fabric of her shoulders. The old woman had spent most of her life caring for her blind and deaf father, the man who tapped the words of his limited vocabulary on the palm of her hand to speak: a tapping she could feel sometimes, even now, when she needed to shift the cloud in her head.

The clouds were dispersing. And there, across the road, was the tallest, demanding that curtis and the girl form a straight line behind him. There he was raising his index finger in the air like a diplomat, shouting.

curtis put his hand over his mouth and chuckled; his shoulders began to move. The tallest pushed him in the ribs, knocking him to the ground. curtis later brought himself to his feet and got back in line. He looked confused, as if he did not understand how laughter could have led to punishment. The girl looked at him. The tallest had dared her to speak, his index finger over her mouth.

The old woman sat on the porch of George's house. The baby had begun to cry. She occasionally reached to the side of her chair and grabbed a bottle of milk, squeezing the rubber nipple to test the temperature of it. When it suited her, she pushed the nipple down the baby's throat, silencing him.

The girl began to scatter, as the tallest counted aloud, his hands over his face. curtis had not run at all. Instead, he stood underneath the oak tree and pointed to an object on a branch. After noticing that no one was paying attention to him, he ran to the porch, where the old woman was now rocking the baby in her bosom. She put the bottle back down beside her and touched curtis on the back with her free hand. He pointed to the oak. The longer it took her to respond, the more impatient he grew with her.

The tallest stopped counting and ran behind the house, until he saw the girl come toward him, stop, and proceed to run again. She was a crooked-faced girl who belonged to the stars. The tallest chased her down and lifted her yellow dress, as he had done many times, pinning her to the side of the house. She tried to push him away but seemed overcome by his strength. He smiled and started to hump her from behind. She was caught up in laughter at first. But as the tallest began to loosen his pants, she stopped smiling and yelled.

It did not matter in Valsin County, Mississippi, who a girl belonged to. Neither did it matter that the blood in your body was as hers, light like hers and running away from something, something tainted. Monstrous. And it was not a child's fault that he did not know who he was or what was born unto him. He was the crooked-letter i of Mississippi.

She was the girl.

And he was the boy.

Same mama, different daddy. And who can apologize for the milk they come from if he has no say-so in how it came to be?

You can call her his sister if you'd like. But in the tallest's mind, he was the son of an elephant. And could not take enough vitamins for the bones in his head to shrink.

She was, simply, the girl.

He stepped away from the girl, his hands over his face. He had long tried to figure out who he was, what he wanted from the Eves of his life. He was an experiment. Everyone was an experiment waiting to sprout on a grand hip of discovery.

The old woman heard the girl scream. She turned away from curtis and walked to the edge of the porch with the baby on her arm. By this time, the tallest had run back behind the house, leaving the girl in tears. The girl then looked up at the old woman, who in a single motion of her hand asked what was wrong. After the girl said nothing, just pulled her dress tail down with one hand over her eye, the old woman demanded that she come to the side of the porch. When the girl made it there, the old woman pointed to her stomach and then to the baby, as if the girl had gotten pregnant simply by the tallest humping her backside.

curtis was back at the oak tree. He looked at the old woman, the way she came down on the girl, then at the baby who had begun to cry loudly.

The tallest came back from around the house: one hand in his back pocket, pigeon-toed and slumped over, active, yellow. Immediately, he noticed curtis at the base of the tree and ran over to him. With a careful eye, he recognized the object and began to search the ground. He ran behind the house and emerged with a big stick. He looked around to see if the old woman had gone inside. Indeed she had. And in her place sat the girl, whose face was hung low, retired.

The tallest pushed curtis out of the way and began to poke at the object. curtis walked backward, looking up, watching as a bird's nest of 360 degrees fell from the branch. The tallest held out his shirt and cradled the nest.

The girl on the porch waited for the old woman to reappear. She would get a beating. She'd be laid down across the bed and her tail would begin to burn, but the old woman would keep going, and then she'd send the girl to the place where girls go when they're dirty: she'd go there, near the bathtub, and cry through the whistling walls, until she'd be told to be quiet, keep her cry way down yonder, so the man could get some sleep.

As she expected, the old woman appeared. Pulled her by the arm and inside the house.

The tallest laughed.

Afterward, curtis tried to touch the pouch of the tallest's shirt where the nest lay. But the tallest turned away from him and raised his index finger again.

George appeared for a moment, her hands at her side, and said nothing before disappearing into the house again. curtis watched the square-shaped pattern above her head turn into vinegar.

His attention was returned to what appeared to be the mother of the nest; she landed on the branch where her baby once was. The tallest saw this and picked up a rock to hit her. Before he had a chance to strike her, she flew away.

In his unbound gravity, the tallest dropped the nest. He looked at his shirt and wiped his hands on the fabric. When he saw what he had done, that one of the eggs had burst on his clothes, he pulled the shirt away from his body, as if he had hoped to find a distant eye floating in the yellow jelly.

But even curtis, with his shadow panting on the ground, knew that the eye had been crushed, as the tallest stood there breathing, the dead matter of a fetus on his hands.

chapter
three

The vein leading up to David's cavity was pulsating. He could feel it pulling out from a hill just below his jawbone and rushing, rushing through the cartilage, past the muscle—it was a muscle sending thunder through an empty cave.

It was gone now.

But he knew there would be a moment when the red would catch up with the blue again and he'd see the vein beating sideways at the edge of his mouth, like the time he asked a man what phosphorus had to do with fire . . . and he breathed from within and lit a match.

chapter four

Too brought her hand to her face: the index finger rested on the tip of her nose. She had begun to close her hand entirely, close it over her breathing body, as if she had seen something, noticed how wind had the capacity to be still. Quiet. The lungs shutting down.

The lungs whispering.

There, in the kitchen window, her hand opened up and the air that had been trapped released itself, as she looked out into the coming of morning, where she swore she had seen a man or animal standing in the sun.

But he was no longer standing.

He was lying sideways.

She opened the door of Logic's bedroom. She had been up since five o'clock: there were yard eggs to find for breakfast and flour to knead for biscuits. She did this for her husband. (Logic had abandoned breakfast altogether. One morning, while helping her mother crack the shells of yard eggs, she found a dead fetus.)

"Get up from there, Logic," she said. "The Missis got some cleaning need doing."

Logic slowly opened her eyes and pulled up the covers, as if the urine in her bladder had leaked out on the sheets. "Okay."

Before Too stepped out of the room, she noticed the staples in Celesta's mouth. Immediately, she ripped her lips apart, saying, "Lawdy be. What you do this here for?"

Logic sat up in bed, the wires of her head reaching for something permanent. "'Cause," she said slowly, "she got butterflies in her stomach too."

A whisper came from her mother's nostrils, like phosphorus burning. "What she got to be nervous about?"

"Lookin' up," said Logic.

The sound of the tallest broke the silence.

"George and her chaps the only folks I know can wake up God," said Too.

But she did not really care about this racket. She was thinking about Logic's vocabulary, how she could talk fully when she wanted to—how she could memorize the music of books under the wind of her tongue where there was a garden of knowledge growing each time she brought home a gift from the Missis.

Just then, Too remembered to ask Logic what she had done to the spines of her books: they were missing, but for the stitching of the binding. She asked.

And Logic answered, "In the closet."

Too hollered for Logic to hurry up from the house. When Logic finally opened the door, she was carrying two iron hangers, one in each hand. Her arms were beside her as she laughed loudly.

"Why you totin' iron?" asked Too.

Logic said nothing, but for her laughter.

The house of the Missis grew closer. It was once an old church; her father had been the pastor for the white folks in town, until he fell ill one evening behind the pulpit and collapsed; no one cried at his funeral, not even his daughter, because she knew where he was going.

Too knocked on the stained-glass window. There was a picture of a lamb grazing. The Missis called down from the top of the stairs—her voice was constantly under construction, as if her vocal cords had become entangled in a web of electricity. Or barbwire.

Too looked up at the Missis, who seemed to have been stirring out of a deep sleep. "Been up all night again, huh?"

The Missis ignored her. "Is that Logic yonder?"

Logic nodded.

The Missis put her delicate hand on the railing and traveled midway down the stairs, her hair the color of freshly stomped wine, her eyes deep in their sockets.

Slated like the bodies of glass marbles: the value of a secret inside.

"Come on up here," she said. "I've been holdin' something for you."

"Okay," Logic said.

Too went into the kitchen. She was arranging cups and saucers to match the blue-rimmed porcelain tiles of the floor. She was careful with her work. Dropping glass was as dangerous as catching babies.

When Logic walked into the Missis' bedroom, she found her sitting on a battered ottoman. "Too told you to leave the hangers outside?" she asked.

Logic nodded.

"Well," said the Missis, "she don't mean nothing by it—thinks I don't like anything that rusts in the rain."

"I know," said Logic.

"You do?" said the Missis, pulling Logic to her, poking her in the side.

"Uh-huh."

She looked down at the Missis' feet. They were veinless. She wondered what had happened to her nerves. Somebody told her that a woman without a map in her feet was running from a dream: courage began when the fetus was asleep in the womb and there was a vertical thread that tied the feet together in order to test the strength of the mind. Everything was connected this way: head to feet, neck to ankles, breasts to abdomen. It is no wonder that when one breaks down, one member of the pair is affected by the other.

The mother of the Missis had moved too much. She could not help it: her feet and hands frozen, her mouth twisted like a blade of grass: involuntary. She had shaken loose the thread in her daughter's feet.

The windows in the room were open. The heat from the earth was almost suffocating. And there on the shelves were the rubies, round cases of perfumed talc, a row of toy soldiers, their faces burned, melted. And up high, two chandeliers, the multifaceted crystal piercing the energy in the room.

The Missis spoke. "What you plan on making with that iron?"

"Wings," said Logic.

The Missis paused and walked over to a vast closet, opening it: "Then I've got just the thing."

Logic ran over to the bed and leaned her upper torso on the down comforter. Her mother yelled up from the kitchen, "You ain't on the Missis' feathers, is you?"

"No," whispered Logic.

She had marked the days of July on Celesta's stomach. July twenty-second, the day she was born to Too and David Harris: nine pounds and nine ounces—headfirst.

The Missis came out of the closet holding a trail of wool. "My daddy killed the lamb that wore this. Might as well use it for angels now," she said.

She believed in God, but only in the existence of dead things.

She had seen Jesus in her dreams, His hand barely lifted above the head of the animal, barely lifted, as if not to intimidate, as if, had the animal begun to bleat, He Himself would have cried.

"A lamb is a trapped child," said the Missis.

Logic touched the Missis' hair and sniffed it.

"You got blood in your hair," she said.

The Missis pulled at her locks. "No," she said. "I like to think of it as ripe fruit."

"Yeah, you do," said Logic. "You got blood in your hair . . . like me."

The Missis laid the wool over Logic's breasts. "Not anymore."

At that moment, they heard the voice of a man who belonged to an unstable world. It was Logic's father.

"He come for me," said Logic.

"I know," said the Missis. Her face seemed motionless; one muscle in her forehead beating like the pulse of helium.

Too called from the kitchen. "Your daddy done come," she said. "Go with 'im. And don't you forget to get that iron off the porch."

The Missis looked down from the window, the freshly stomped wine in her hair bottling the flat air around her, as Logic and her father walked back down through the trees—the wool folded neatly over the rods of iron.

chapter
five

He laid her on the operating table.

Logic had been in her room picking up a drawing of the tallest's stomach that she had found while walking the path to her house; he had painted it green, the intestines a bright orange, and where his name was supposed to be he put *pituitary*, as if he could not distinguish one gland of his fragile body from another. Logic pasted it to her mirror and began to touch her belly, which was now beginning to form a small pouch.

Her father had stepped into the house.

She had known his routine: stiffen his shoulders at the door's opening, walk toward the faucet with one hand on his gut, and sigh deeply before putting the gun in the kitchen window—always putting the gun somewhere.

Always loaded.

Always, always loaded.

He knew that Too was with the Missis tonight and made his way to Logic's bedroom. He remembered the scent of Logic's open mouth at birth. Like vinegar.

He had long stopped touching Too. He had gained weight and told her that his belly would crush her. But Too did not believe this. She had felt the ovaries of crushed women. Women like George, whose body was jelly. Or kerosene.

It was not hard to take Logic away from ordinary things. She was a child who always paid attention. Because no one expected her to.

One tap on the shoulder, near the collarbone, and Logic followed her father into the operating room. He lit a candle; the flame rose upward, the hips of it floating, as if it were a child being baptized.

Logic was not afraid of light.

God had cut the moon down the center; a crooked line moved through her body. There it was. There it was again. It was traveling through bone. She lifted her fingers to hold it, the crooked line. But even this, her grasp, could not stop it from evaporating.

Logic was naked now.

Her body was even thinner these days. Were you sitting on the limb of a widespread tree, you could have looked down upon her as a thin paragraph; she was solemn yet powerful this way; the value of her near-weightless body carried a number of adjectives around, tucked in her belly.

She could have used them, shouted them out, had he sat still long enough to catch them.

David walked around the operating table. His hands dirty. His jawbone shaped like the hoof of some animal, a raw-edged catastrophe, when he swallowed. So much had gone down into the gut of David Harris, in no particular order: his mother, who died with a tiny blue purse in her hand; a nest of bird's eggs he had caught and crushed with the heel of his foot; a seahorse. And those other digestable images that went through his body and disappeared like living acid.

Logic was not there in the room with him. She was in the tallest's pituitary gland, following a trail of blood that emptied out into a field of green. The tree was there, in the center, lopsided. And there was a child like her, thin like her, crawling upward— up to the very top. Logic saw where the wings were beginning to form on her spine. There above each was a piece of iron—like a tiny horseshoe—at the base of her neck where for many seasons she had been unable to lift her head because she could not smile into bone.

The rising smoke of the candle treaded the air. David gathered himself. He had called on God many times before taking his penis out of Logic's vagina. She wished he had said it this way: vagina, the scientific way.

But he did not.

He said pussy.

chapter
six

Too Harris had somewhere to be. She was a mechanism.

Tic. Toc. Tic. Toc. There it went again, accompanied by the sound of a child screaming across the road. But she could not think of children at this moment, as much as she could not balance her body on this floor. With this heel. Or this foot.

She was not only a mechanism but an appointment. Her head set to the twelve o'clock position, as if she were destined to arrive, in her mind, at midnight. Or noon.

Pitiful Too Harris.

Pitiful Too Harris.

She was as loose as dust drifting, as loose as dust crumbling.

Over there, near the window, she touched the fat of her eye. The pupil turned into a shadow when her finger blocked her vision. But she could feel nothing really: for nothing, not even an atom, wanted her. And she, in the drought of her wilted body, wanted nothing in return.

Tic Toc. Tic Toc.

Again, she could hear it. A mammal of some kind was nagging her, calling her Mama. She could only imagine she had not said it loudly enough in her head: she did not want to think of children, not now, when she had no understanding of the word.

She herself was vaporized.

George should have kept that chap quiet. She could hear the tallest screaming to the very top of his lungs. The vibration went down inside his agile body and turned into something cold.

Mama, he said.

Mama.

Too turned away from this boy in his boy's body.

The ticking stopped.

She could sit down now. A time or two she'd miss the noon appointments in her body and have to wait till midnight to make up for it. She did not mind. Where did she really have to be?

Wherever it was it would send her a notice. And she'd sit awhile. But then . . . but then, she'd go.

chapter
seven

David had gone to Pyke County, the next town over, when Logic opened the door of her mother's bedroom. Too was reading one of the Missis' diaries; it was open in her lap, the pages thin like the veins of a trembling hand.

Too had heard the Missis say something the night she had slept in her house: the Missis had been crying uncontrollably when Too asked her if it was the devil she saw when the moon was split open.

Her answer was an adjective followed by a long word.

She often memorized the expression on the Missis' face when saying things: her relaxed tongue, the bridge of her upper jaw absent any sign of bone, as if it had been bound for attention.

Logic sat beside Too in bed.

Too looked up from the pages. "What's in your head now, Logic?"

"Blood."

Too sat up in the bed and parted Logic's hair. But there was nothing to find. She had gotten all the blood out long ago; the wound had closed up. She knew this but had somehow wondered if her skull had been cracked from the eardrum.

"Must be the blood o' Jesus," said Too.

Logic stood up for a moment. She had been up through the night, lying naked on the bathroom floor, trying to find her pituitary gland in her stomach. She thought that perhaps she could paste it to the picture drawn by the tallest. One clip of the gland, some fresh cotton and alcohol to cleanse the wound. Surely, she would not have felt it. Things go back to where they come from. She had felt this gland shrinking inside her; it was quiet. Perhaps, if it had made a peculiar noise, moved, she could have pulled it out of her body. She listened for it—but nothing. No sound. She washed her hands repeatedly; it was the germs of her father's semen that had caused the gland to shrink.

She put her fingers over Too's face.

"Quit," said Too. "I shoulda left your head open. Maybe then you'd have the sense the good Lawd gave you."

Logic showed no response. She walked over to the large metallic fan in the window and put her face up to the blade. The heat of the earth was in her nostrils now, and she could hear the tallest telling his siblings what to do. Not only could she hear this, but the sound of her mother's breathing; she was an open wire.

A green lamp sat beside her mother's bed: David's fingerprints, like floating mollusks, coated the picture above their faces. His mother was holding a blue purse. There was a silver ball to open it, an intimate clip to confine it. This woman's eyes were lively: nothing of paranoia or distance.

Logic disappeared from the window. She began to laugh, her hands on her belly.

"What you laughing at now?" asked Too.

Immediately, without any pressure on her lungs, Logic whispered, "You."

*　*　*

When David returned home, Too was in the kitchen lighting a rectangular box of redheaded matches. She peered out at the tallest and suddenly remembered the time when she was a little girl and almost knocked her breath out.

"Hungry?" asked Too.

It was not unusual for him to avoid her. She knew he did not care to see her naked, and it drove a web of silence between them.

"Got some rutabagas going," said Too.

Silence.

Too was a spear. The space around her was suffocating. She herself was inanimate and often dreamed of herself without anyone attached to her ribs—husband or child.

David looked at the tallest, who was on the side of his house humping a slave; the tallest had made a slave of this creature, wrapped it in fishing twine, the elbows behind its back, the midsection bare. David watched him do this and put his weak arms on his stomach; it was impossible for him to tell whether the creature was a boy or girl. He himself was pitiful; he wished he had the honesty of the tallest, the untamed habit of doing things openly. "Sissy," he said, before walking down the hall, past the operating room, where the candle had gone out.

chapter
eight

Logic was walking on the path to her house when she heard a voice from up high. "Where you been?"

It was the tallest. His body was a trapezoid, his shoulders forward. He was bare-chested, his nipples swollen as if they had been filled with milk. "You hear me?" he asked.

Logic looked up at him and pointed to the multicolored map in her hand. "Dakota."

"Dakota?" asked the tallest. "North or South?"

Logic shrugged her shoulders and an answer she was unsure of emerged. "North, I reckon."

"Shit," said the tallest, "you don't even know ups from downs. Reckon you'd piss on yourself if a ghost come running."

Logic put the map on the ground and watched a june bug crawl up her leg. "How come?"

The tallest leaned back against the tree; the bones in his forehead protruded outward. His head was a tornado up close. "'Cause that mean you don't know God from hell."

Logic was carrying the blue purse that had once belonged to her grandmother. It was the second gift given to her by her father; she awoke to find him sitting on the edge of her bed, his hands vibrating.

The tallest immediately jumped down from the branch. "Let me see that," he said.

Logic paid him no mind; she was busy looking at the language of colors on the map, her fingertips traveling downward.

The tallest opened the mouth of the purse and pulled out the broad-shouldered strap: "This here where your words go?"

Logic hissed at him. "Sometimes."

He danced around her. "You don't even talk in a straight line."

"So."

"My mama got shoes this color, but she say they ain't no good for folks who talk crooked," he said.

"How come?"

"'Cause," said the tallest, "you either one way or the other. Up or down."

Logic laughed. "Unless you got butterflies in your stomach."

"Well," said the tallest, "I ain't scared o' nothin' in public. And I ain't hiding 'less I got something to hide from."

"Like the world?"

The tallest laid the blue purse down beside her and began to walk away, his quiet footsteps in a perfect row. "Yeah," he said. "Like the world."

When Too made it home, the stars were beginning to align themselves in a shapeless vocabulary in the sky. She looked toward the house of the tallest, whose mother, George, was lying on the front porch with a man inside of her.

"David?" she said, when she opened the front door.

He was sitting at the kitchen table in the dark, breathing unsteadily.

"What's the matter wit'chu?" asked Too.

"Nothing," he said.

She went to kiss him, but he moved away from her as if she were acid.

"All right."

She went to the bedroom. His shirt was still wet with sweat. She picked it up, as if it were a child, and folded it over the windowsill to dry. She remembered the last time they slept together: the upright position of his jawbone, the wings of a mobile creature floating in the air beneath the hollering locusts in the darkness.

David was drunk when she sat on top of him.

She took his penis and leaned her body forward, rising only a little to come down upon it, so it could open her up from the inside. But it did not matter.

At that moment it was not him but the man in the corner of the room, the imaginary one, who was penetrating her.

chapter
nine

George's face was random.

She was in need of company; you could look underneath the bottom lid of her eye and tell it; she had not been sleeping in her house. There shone an imbalanced pitch where she had been trying to speak and the diction, the loose balance of her vocabulary, could not hold, when it was her face that had lost gravity.

She looked down at the dress she had been wearing. How could even a child describe the way in which she wore it, the idle colors drooping forward from the basic pattern that had been battered, strewn across the fabric, as if panting, saying quickly to the shadow on the ground: you are a beast and I am falling apart. For a time, she appeared uncomfortable in the dress, as if she would reach for it down near the hem and pull it over her head, abandon it in dust.

She had carried children in her stomach, most of them crushed by the weight of a man on her ovaries. She looked out across the road, where Too was braiding Logic's hair, and walked toward her, a glass of ice water in her hand.

She was on the porch of Too's house now, the heat rising from the earth, as she watched the shadow move alongside the edge of the house, lift its arm to swallow a cube from the glass that had begun to melt in the soaring heat around her.

She spoke. "I can't breathe."

If George had been made of something insistent, a photograph, a radio, jolting electricity, Too Harris could have sat her near the rim of a lake, pushed her from behind, and waited for her to drown.

"And you mean every word of it," said Too. "Don't you?"

She had saved and buried most of George's babies, the eggs suffocating.

George realized, during the silence of her activity, that she had survived many wars. Just then, in one great big hurry, she had seen herself walk away from Too, Logic, and the singular blade of grass that she had pressed down with her foot; she was preparing herself for the customer. He could stick his penis inside her if he wanted. But she would not feel it. He could lay her in the trenches, muddy up her hair, for he did not know that the fighting of a prostitute lies in the shadow on the ground.

The sound of the ice cubes melting brought her to. She picked up the transparent glass and shook it. "Thirsty."

Too ran her fingers over the scar in Logic's head and felt the mass of flesh there; it was permanent. And when she realized its permanency, she thought of how her mother had split her stomach in two to remove Logic from her umbilical cord; her water bag had burst and she did not want her to drown.

George leaned back against the wooden column. Her pores were open, the scent of the lost babies rising up from her vagina. "Do you think of love?"

"No," said Too.

George smiled and cleared her throat, the lump falling downward, as if she could have been born a man. "It's all around."

She paused for a moment and looked across the road; the laughter of her children permeated the air, alive. Logic could always find the tallest. He was becoming a part of her; she'd touched his pituitary gland in the mirror and felt she had found a small batch of field peas in his intestines.

curtis was at the base of the tree: his fingers were spread apart in front of him. They balanced him somehow, his face still trembling from a hard fall, the girl behind him.

George rose and picked up the glass at her feet. "I best be going now," she said. "He got a storm brewing."

And she walked away from the house, a silent wind picking up the hem of her dress.

Too was still out on the porch when David came home. He had stopped for a moment, under the broken shadow of the moon, and thrust his hips back, his hands beside him. The things he did in silence: the slumped backbone, the nostrils flaring widely.

Lightning bugs were swarming around him. He opened his mouth as if to say something, and Too saw the raw light go down his throat. He swallowed it.

Upon realizing this, he brought his hands up to his neck and spat on the ground. He had begun to have nightmares: his kidney had been punctured—a winding river of blood dripped down near his ribs; he had been lying on his stomach, his penis erect, until the river flooded him out from inside and there it was before him— the blade of the paring knife.

The light was stuck in his throat. He walked toward the porch, where Too was standing with a glass of cold milk in her hands. "Here," she said.

He pushed her to the side, saying, "You think 'cause I give you a rib you got rights to me?"

Too said nothing.

"I'm whole on the inside," he continued.

He went for the bottle beneath his bed, a smooth cognac. There was a time when he had drunk among men, until he had begun to notice how quickly they deteriorated before him: the explosion of one man's liver, another with a set of broken molars from when he had fallen under a streetlight in New Orleans, the tattooing of the name that he had been called his entire life: sissy.

And the man who tried to kill him.

But he could not think about this. Not now.

He could hear Logic on the other side of the wall. She was talking to God. And he, like Too, was bothered by her constant humming—for she breathed this way the many nights he lay on top of her in the operating room. What would it be like to cut her open from the inside? he thought. Where did this music come from? Perhaps, he imagined, an ant crawled into her head as she lay under the big oak tree, half dead. It was tapping on her nerves now—and he had heard a man at the woodyard swear that the doctors up north put animals on metal tables and split them open—one tap or clenching of a nerve with a pair of tweezers and another until they were solid upstairs.

There it was again—this sound. The liquor was beginning to dizzy him. Too was in the bathroom; she had taken the record player from an old closet, and he knew she had the Johnsons. Her fingers were on the head of her clitoris and a stream of milk was coming out of her. It was he, Robert Johnson, who had given her the juice.

The humming . . . the humming . . . again. He reached for the bedpost and pulled himself up. Surely he had felt the lightning bug at the back of his throat. He opened his wide mouth and stuck his finger underneath the flap there; he did not want this light inside of him. He thought it would ignite the sin in him. Of course, he knew that he was walking kerosene.

Logic's voice grew gentler. Had she known or cared that he was just behind her, she would have felt the need for protection. But Logic was not a violent child. Rarely did she ever push him away when he entered her body.

She could hold water.

David stood behind her, his hands open; he could have killed her.

He could have flattened this noise, this music from the child who knew more of who she was—with the scar on her head—than he had ever known in being alive.

He had come so close to strangling her, his hands a short distance from the life in her body, until he saw the doll: he had seen her in his nightmares without any staples to keep her quiet.

chapter
ten

He is that he was.

chapter
eleven

The tallest looked out of the square-shaped window of his shotgun house; everyone was gone—only a trail of his mother's perfume settling on the rays of heat around him. His bedroom was at the back of the house, near the kitchen. There were nights when his mother would send for him. She wanted her back lyed down; he had knelt behind her many times, the towel wringing in his hands, as the water dripped down around her neck and onto her swollen breasts. He had drawn her entire anatomy on a piece of cardboard; it took him one full summer to divide the bones from the muscles, the arteries from the singular and plural pronouns on his grammar sheet. A woman was scientific. He had convinced himself of it.

He had been to the city once in his life. And it was there, on a street named Common, that he saw a crowd of punks carrying a department store mannequin. He followed them to a junkyard of old cars—clearly, he had heard one of them say that women get pregnant by men who swallow avocados. This did not matter; he had long discovered, at an early age, the chemistry of the human body. It confused him. He could not figure out whether he was more inclined to man or the thought of having a woman in his genes: he had to choose.

One of the boys pulled a switchblade out of his pocket and cut a hole between the mannequin's legs. The others laughed at this. The boy put the knife back into his pocket and pushed the mannequin's legs upward. Then he pulled down his pants—his penis was uncircumcised. The others turned around as he climbed on top of the mannequin and fucked her until his penis began to bleed; she had cut him.

He grabbed hold of the earth beside him, and when the other boys saw the blood come out of his flesh, they ran.

The tallest sat there for hours, waiting for the boy to leave her side. He would remember him forever—never would he forget what a rapist looked like: the salt of his pores, the unbridled eyes, without regret or Moses or the man who sent him.

Once the mannequin was in his hands, he balanced her on the ground.

He was in his bedroom now. Behind him were various books on numerology and the body and its uses. Now, both the victim and the books were in the center of the floor. He had given this woman no true identity; it was no she or he. It was simply—a victim.

On more than one night, he had filled his bed with urine. He was afraid to go to the bathroom alone. It was the familiarity of his mother's voice that had comforted him. Because he had heard his mother scream loudly—heard her say once: *No*.

He walked past the room curtis shared with the girl: the scribbled drawing of a cucumber, saturated, beside her bed. He was in his mother's bedroom now. She had saved the picture of the Italian philosopher he had given her, the one who had taught him what hell looked like. There, lifeless on the chifforobe, was the dress.

He liked being naked when walking privately around the house. He lifted his arms and slid the fabric down over his chest. He was his mother now, George. The heat came up from the wooden boards below him—he reached for his testicles, his penis, and pushed them between his thighs, hiding them.

Everyone told him, women mostly, that he looked like George, he had eyes like George, that George must've spat him out at birth, but no one had ever told him how much he had to prove, to admit about who and what he was.

No one knew how frightened he was. It was not men he hated. It was totalitarianism. Without argument, part of him was a boy. Boys curse others with what they hate most about the world.

He had heard the voices of men in his house, how they'd suc-cumbed to the Adam's apples in their throats, and spent an entire night touching his larynx for fear that his syllables would come out heavy because the pressure of becoming a man would subject him to it. There was a pattern that men followed. They looked for the hairs of their chests to sprout and dreamed of women coming down from strange mountains.

He touched his forehead and wondered how long it would take for the swelling to go down. He was an elephant.

The makeup powder was before him. He pressed the sponge against his face, under the eyes. In doing so, he had discovered the particles rising above him; they were the atoms of a prostitute. He was well aware of his mother's activities. But he had also seen her on her knees at night, asking God to forgive her; it was her chil-dren she hoped to save.

But when alone, there was no totalitarian within him or the world around him. It was safe to close his eyes and scrape the packed eye shadow; he blew the broken debris away from the brush. And closed one eye to outline his lid in what was the vessel of his mother's work.

And there, on the end table beside her bed, was the wig. She wore it for even the poorest customer: a woman should always feel priceless regardless of her surroundings. He pulled it off the head of the Styrofoam bust; the smell of artificial things made him crave the taste of silence, honesty. What was unreal was blind—and blind, beautiful.

There it was, the lipstick. He was not ready for this. He formed a muscle with his hand and watched it ride the radius of his arm. A woman he had seen while traveling—half asleep—dragged her baby by one arm. Her muscle was like his, going up, complacent. Had he pursed his lips, brought the redness to his mouth, the memory of the woman . . . he didn't know. He was thinking of something else now, a puppy that swallowed a five-dollar bill.

He looked at himself in the mirror again. No one would ever touch him again. He was not made of plastic or music. He was made of confusion, the son of an elephant.

There, holding the red in his hands, he put the words of his head on the mirror: *This is the last time you will ever get this close to me.*

And then, as if set to a score or nerve, he lay down on his mother's bed, wondering if he would smear these words or memorize them.

chapter
twelve

Celesta had begun to wilt in the corner of Logic's room. Logic had become afraid to touch her. On instinct, she listened for a grave noise to come from her stomach: a tulip sprouting.

A lamb bleating.

Logic had touched Celesta by accident; she thought she'd felt a bone setting back inside her shoulder. Something about the doll had become dislocated since the night Logic heard the creeping of footsteps behind her. Logic had been telling things to God. You can never imagine what one says to God when adamant. Perhaps she liked the teasing of death at her shoulders. Perhaps she thought Celesta would answer her, eventually.

Too was gone to pull a baby out of a woman's vagina. She had left a photograph of sin on the table. Two bodies. Two parts of the anatomy: lust.

When Logic discovered it, she folded it into a square. Burned it.

The tallest was in his yard, his siblings around him, pointing to the limb where the mother of the eggs had flown away. He opened his hands and looked at his fingers. Closed them. Opened them again. When curtis walked up to him, he began to label each finger: the index was up high. He explained the others like clay under fire.

A man pulled up in his yard. He was stiff, as if he was made of paper. He tested the space around him. curtis ran up to him, checking his pockets for money. But he did not respond; he cared less about the movement of creatures. He lived in a place separate from the laughter of children and angels.

"Where your mama?" he asked.

curtis pointed to the open door of the house. George appeared barefoot. She leaned her head against the wooden frame. If there was fear in her, it was gone. She had seen men like the man made of paper and others, made of other things, and there was no difference in the way they parked their cars, the obedience they subjected her children to, or the outline of their frozen voices in the darkness. Her life was in the penis of them all.

The man-made-of-paper smiled and took a number of coins from his pocket. curtis opened the palm of his hand and counted them, hiding them from the others. George walked to the center of the porch and paused. "A man still pays for kindness," she said.

The tallest did not care about the money from the man-made-of-paper. He sat on the bark of the tree and looked out, away from the running girl around him. He was connected to this house. He was still here, tangled.

George took the man-made-of-paper's hand and walked through the door of her house, closing it behind her.

Logic walked toward the tree, but stopped, when she heard the sound of dust coming up from the earth. A strange car was driving up the road. And she hated it, because she would rather have been thinking of babies.

It was a Ford. The woman driving was dead. Her shoulders were erect and she wore a yellow hat with a thin layer of lace around it. Her mouth was almost transparent. What use was it? Logic thought.

She had seen a mouth like hers in comic books with the depth of a razor blade.

The car stopped in front of her house.

The woman turned her head to the side and grabbed something from the seat beside her. She was a healthy woman. There were no brown spots in her eyes, nothing tired about her. Her skin was clean, flawless. "How're you this afternoon?" she asked.

Logic sat down in the dust.

The woman was holding papers. She did not know that Logic was distrustful of people who held things in their hands too long, things that were patterns.

"Your folks home?" asked the woman.

Logic shook her head.

The woman continued. "I sell insurance."

Logic began to draw words in the dust. She occasionally looked up at the woman to see if she had turned away. But she had not; she was watching the tallest at the root of the oak tree, his head between his knees.

"What for?" asked Logic.

The woman was pleased that she had said something. "'Cause people die."

"How much is it?" asked Logic.

"What?"

"Death," said Logic.

The woman put the papers on the hood of the Ford and took off her watch to hold them down. "Well," she said, "it depends."

"You gotta be rich to die?" asked Logic.

"Not necessarily," said the woman. "Prepared, at least."

Logic lay on her stomach now. She had drawn a box around her letters. The closer the woman grew to her, the more she guarded the letters with her arms. "Prepared . . . prepared," Logic repeated.

The tallest climbed atop the man-made-of-paper's car. The old woman had arrived on the porch, yelling for him to get down. He slid down from the machine before dissolving altogether.

"My mama's at the Missis'," said Logic.

The woman went back to the hood of the car and picked up her watch. "Where's that?"

"Up the road a piece," said Logic, pointing past the large oak tree.

And so the sun began to move, as it would move in this direction tomorrow, when no one would come, at this hour, to see how far it crept up beyond the unclear range of a sleeping cloud.

"Mighty welcome," said the woman. She wanted to open the door of the Ford, steady her pitiful hand on the seat beside her, but she was compelled, wanted to say, if only now and never again, "I didn't get your name."

"I know," said Logic. "'Cause I ain't dead yet."

The man-made-of-paper emerged from the open door of George's house. The tallest stood behind him, made a gun with his fingertips, and blew his brains out.

chapter thirteen

Logic had piled a load of her mother's sheets in her arms and walked out the back door. The washbasin was filled with hot water and there was a table beside it; her father had been hunting. He had killed a rabbit.

Logic had spent the morning hours looking at her index finger. There was a clot of blood underneath the skin. She had gone to pick up the Bible and felt the open pain of a sewing needle going through her finger. She made no noise at all but had turned around to see a trail of blood growing at her feet like the sharpness of vertebrae.

Now, looking at this redness, how the blood was turning midnight before her, she began to laugh. She could feel her lungs opening up, wondered how they seemed to pulsate with the earth around her. There, up high, where God was, she would need no insurance or men made of paper. And as she breathed, the two pulses began to form an action verb.

She began to lay the sheets out on the washboard. They were the color of angels at one time, the white ones that fly in books, but the pressure of loneliness had turned them yellow. She felt the stiffness of her mother's face as she touched the fabric. With her hand underneath it, she saw the fragile muscles rise with the movement of her fingers. And when she made a fist, she imagined the long wire of the jawbone being crushed.

She had wished, sometimes, that both Too and David were powder. Then they would be at her mercy. And she could lay them out on the wind like sheets, to dry in the heat and blow them away.

A sharp line of pain rushed through her lower back. The butterflies were becoming heavy now. She walked away from the sheets and held herself up beside the table where the dead rabbit lay still. She looked at it, this thing, and touched its flesh.

"Get away from there," said David. "Ain't you got work to do?"

He walked up behind her, his hand on her back where the pain had yawned in her kidneys.

The action verb was gone.

She wanted the universe to hear this sound: her father had crushed the skull of the rabbit against the tree behind her. Now he was splitting it down the middle, chest to groin. He stuck his finger inside the opening and pulled its intestines out.

There, coming around the side of the house, was the tallest. He was barefoot. He had taken his vitamins for the afternoon; he yet hoped that the bones in his forehead would shrink.

There were times when he seemed intimidated by David. But there were others when he did not care about the voices of human beings because he had seen what they were made of. He looked at Logic and laughed. But it was not really Logic he was laughing at, it was the man who made her.

He ran up to David and stopped just shy of the tree, leaning on the side where the intestines seemed to have been crawling, alive. "How you cook your kill?" he asked.

David looked at him as if he wished it were his skull he had crushed. "I don't," said David. "That's for the womenfolks to do."

The tallest mocked him. He repeated this line a number of times with his hands on his hips. David watched him. The sharp blade in his hands could have gutted his laughter, muzzled the violins in his throat.

Within an instant, the tallest stopped his mocking. But he was not concerned with death. He had become numb to men and their voices. "I just come for sugar," he said.

David looked over at Logic, who had begun to hang the first sheet out on the line. She wiped her hands on her clothes and started for the house. The tallest followed her, as he put his hand over his clavicle.

She was just over the stove when the tallest began to breathe heavily. He sat down on the floor beside her and listened to the sound of sugar filling glass. "That lady come over to my house last summer," he said. "But she wouldn't sell my mama no insurance for dead folks."

Logic stared at him. "Why?"

"'Cause she said her name George," he said. "And she could get mixed up with a soldier."

Logic looked down at his feet. The arch shifted upward. The heel was solid, steady. She put a lid on the jar and handed it to him. He jumped up off the floor and touched her stomach.

She let him.

He touched her face and saw the language of hunger. Food was a terrible thing to put in her mouth, when she was so cold inside, so filled. Her arms were delicate like a parasite in darkness. The tallest put his eardrum to her abdomen; he could hear the rhythm of floating activity, as he had the men in his mother's bedroom.

"You better feed them butterflies if you want to go to heaven," he said, grabbing the sugar out of her hands.

She watched him walk away, the arch in his feet picking up a row of dust behind him.

Too was in the bathroom mirror. She had gotten something caught in her eye. She wet the tip of her finger and pulled up her eyelid. It was clear.

Too could hear Logic on the front porch moving Celesta around. The noise stopped.

There was a transparent line on her fingertips.

The sun was going down. She did not have the Johnsons now, but her womb was vibrating. She picked up a portable mirror and looked at her clitoris. She was mesmerized by it; the temple that surrounded it bound her to what she was. She lifted it and began to press down on the feeling beneath it. She was Logic's age when she found it and had become addicted to having a warm hand on its matter, until the liquid opened her body and let the scent of the earth out of her.

She remembered being in her mother's bathwater, how the fumes from her ovaries rose upward. There were tiny hair follicles floating around her. She picked them up. She was holding life inside her hands. Each night, she did this. She looked for life in her mother's bathwater and wondered where they came from, if there was a disciple beneath the pores of her flesh passing out seeds of growth. She would look up at her mother; her own vagina was closing up again.

The opening as tight as silk, the hairs around it framed in solitude.

Her flat feet on wood.

Her spine almost extinct.

Because it was not the living things that were alive, but the objects of a woman's house.

logic

*   *   *

The front door opened; she could hear Logic walk into her bedroom now, putting Celesta in the corner. There were many nights
when Too herself had felt the doll was human. Logic would be in
one part of the house and Too would be putting her nightgown
on her dresser. It was Too who held Celesta in her hands and
searched for a beating heart. A pulse. Then she would leave her
in the corner, never lifting Celesta's dress to search for the ripped
clitoris.

Logic began to hum. When Too opened the door, she found
her standing in the window. Her face was a cloud of activity, the
nose coming down crookedly over her mouth, the chin like a
square root, her head upright, as if she had ruled it.

"That racket," said Too.

The jagged line of the moon was evaporating: there behind the
skull of the rabbit where the eyes had been gouged out.

Dead now.

chapter
fourteen

When you open your mouth, you're supposed to lay your words down till they look like something innocent. Or guilty.

chapter
fifteen

The man was an atom.

David was not thinking of the man, not really, but the sound of his index finger in a glass of ice cubes. Cold.

Where was he?

The music was so disturbing. Somebody—anybody—take David Harris home. The bodies before him, rotating around him, were shapeless. Where was Too?

Had he not been sitting at this jook joint, all the unfamiliar faces around him, he would not have asked for her. His temples pulsated so very quickly. He could have broken skin, split the side of his head open, and let the red breathe for a while. He could do nothing with it: trapped there, as if welded to the skull, the muscle moving forward only to land in an uneven place, where it could split David Harris in two.

His hand, airless on the table, was bound by something invisible: magic, he hoped—could not stop the world from spinning. Not even the drunkard with a missing bone in his nose or the rectangular jukebox—of which he had seen in shadows, darkness. Not even the woman with the blue purse; she could have been his mother.

All these things, at intervals, circling him in a place with no name, because he had wandered far enough from the woodyard to find himself at the edge of a leaping vein.

Moving, without question, without him.

Through him.

The man was invisible.

David Harris was not.

Somebody tell me where I am? he whispered, his head low.

No one answered. He could hear the man shouting. David Harris could not see the world he had put himself in from the outside.

And the others: their faces turning away, turning to stone, as if the presence of something greater—a greater degree, perhaps—had made it that way.

Then, at that moment, David Harris heard it: *click!*

Before he emerged from the frozen sheets, Too permanent, like scribbled ink, beside him.

chapter

sixteen

Logic was in the Missis' bedroom, bending hangers for her wings. The Missis herself was naked. Her breasts were deformed, her waist meek. The fur between her legs went up from her abdomen in a column of darkness. Logic had always wondered if the wine-colored hair on her head matched that of her down-below. It did not. And she sat there watching her move lightly across the floor, her fingers occasionally stretching upward where there was nothing to grasp but silence.

The Missis could not help but think of her mother while in this position. Now, with her fingers this way, straight and forward, as if a tiny thread had been knotted at the bone and a child were pulling her, forcing her to vibrate.

The Missis turned away from Logic; she did not want her to see the sharp parting of her lips where the air was beginning to slow down, detach itself from her face. She could feel Logic moving around, and with this sound she remembered the morning of her mother's death.

Yes, she remembered; there was a disturbance in her mother's brain. The red in her veins caught up with the blue and her mouth became twisted. Her hands frozen. Her feet frozen.

Involuntary.

The Missis had seen it in her dreams, how the drowning occurred: her mother was in the porcelain bathtub when it happened, her head sideways, her body ticking and tocking, until the red began to shout. And she heard it. She heard it and could not call out. Could not say to anyone: hope me. The waters rose in the porcelain: she could hear the Missis, her only child, dangling from the limbs of the oak tree, U-shaped.

It was the tree that saved the Missis from finding the body.

The mouth twisted.

The hands frozen.

The feet frozen.

A child knows not, upon play, when her mother is drowning.

The Missis turned over to look at Logic, her long arms over the sheets. "I saw a star last night," she said. "I thought of you."

Logic smiled.

The Missis touched her wine-colored hair and coiled it around her fingertips. She soaked it in mud each morning. She wanted the scent of the earth in it.

"I'll pay you ten cents to ring the bells at dusk," she said to Logic.

She wanted to hear the sound of redemption.

"Okay," said Logic. She did not care for money. She wanted to disturb.

The Missis got up and looked out into her yard. Too was lying on her side, the summer wind exposing her backside. She did not care that Too read her diaries.

She touched the freckles on her face. They formed a galaxy. And there, hidden behind the hairs of her abdomen, was another she had found by accident.

"Do you think I'm brave?" she asked Logic, who was now twisting the iron arc of the hangers and putting them aside.

Logic looked at her, the disturbed serenity in her body, and answered, "No."

The Missis hoped that someone would tell her the truth. She loved the voices of children, because they were not able to tell honesty from a lie unless threatened. "How come?"

Logic ignored her for a moment; she was tired of always being questioned. Grown-ups always wanted to know where the blade of their consciousness could be measured. Then, after the iron arc of the fourth hanger was decapitated, she replied, "'Cause you scared o' lightning."

"It's not lightning that I'm afraid of," said the Missis. "It's electricity."

"Same thing," Logic snapped.

The Missis posted herself against the headboard of the bed.

Her hands shook.

The room was bland at first. Logic saw a toy soldier that had been sitting at the edge of the bed. The melted face. The cold eye. Only a hole the size of a sewing needle between the lips.

Catastrophic.

She breathed into the face.

The plastic lung whistled. Soon, Logic realized, that it was not the plastic lung, but the cold eye where a vein had burst behind the pupil. As inconsistent, dead as this thing was, it had to breathe.

The Missis' hand opened where Logic had now lain the toy soldier. Her fingers closed over the body, the face, where she felt, at this moment, the warmth of Logic's breath on the vein. Her oxygen had turned to sweat.

Logic then picked up the spool of fishing twine she had brought from her house. She pushed it through the eye of the needle and stacked the hangers around her. One center to another, until they formed triangular patterns, sideways, one on top of the other, one beneath the other. And there, at the curved centers, she began to stitch the foundation of the wings. She remembered her mother sitting at her bedside; her spirit rose as Too lifted the skin of her head and bridged the aisle in her scalp. This is how she stitched the iron together, until she saw the spine of the butterfly surface.

"Now," said the Missis, "all you need is feathers."

The sun shone down on her pubic hairs. They sat up high between her thighs. The pain traveled around her. It was in her system. Had she been made of plastic, she would have been sitting in the room of the tallest with a jagged hole between her legs. But she had, indeed, been as lacerated as the mannequin. Perhaps the mannequin had more control over her inanimate body than this woman—for the Missis did not cut the man who took her; she was of flesh and it was flesh and rib and bone that violated her.

Logic picked up the wings and put them over the Missis' face.

The Missis lay there, her eyes closed.

Her mouth crooked.

chapter
seventeen

The right side of David's face was swollen. Something in the woodyard had bitten him, and he walked home with a set of orange antennae embedded under his skin. Too laid him down on the operating table and pulled them out with a pair of tweezers.

Now he stood up from the bed and touched his face. He felt the poison pulsating in his eardrum. Whatever it was, it had caught him off balance. If only he had seen it, crushed it with his hands. The poison . . . the poison was circulating now and he could feel himself growing a fever. He sat back down on the bed and waited for the world to stop spinning.

He called for Too. She was in the backyard showing the ex-con the land that he was supposed to barbwire. He was fresh from the stone jungle; a group of numbers had cornered him. His body was loose then, so it was easy for him to be reached from the outside. The numbers flooded him with milk and left him open from behind; it was the loneliest measurement of his life. He had been raised by women, always surrounded by their perfumes and their high-heeled voices under a full moon. They had taught him the patterns of the earth and the connection of his body to animals, nature. It was not the fault of womankind—for women were raised

in transparent dangers. They were not schooled on rape and sui-
cide, crime. It was in them to become paralyzed after being poi-
soned, because they had arrived on a limb of naïve tranquillity.
The ex-con thought of them at this moment, as he touched the
cracked rib at his side; it was shaped like a canine tooth in his
intestines.

Too ignored David's callings and watched the ex-convict move
closer to the land around them. His head was a giant telescope;
she had seen one of those things in a magazine. A man stood over
it with his eye up to the glass. The word CONSTELLATIONS was written in big letters, and the inscription under the man said that
Russia had the same moon as America.

"How much it gone cost me?" asked Too.

The ex-con looked at her imperfect mouth and said, "Nothing."

"But I'd hate for you to do all this—"

"Don't worry 'bout pay," said the ex-con. "God send me where
He want me."

Too hushed.

The ex-con continued. "And I don't ask no questions."

She had felt a candle burning inside of him, as it had the night
she had stayed with the Missis, burning brightly above an object
or two, dictated by a breath or an answer.

David had found his way to the back door of the house: he saw
Too there, talking to the ex-con, her hands relaxed on her hips,
unbridled. "Can't you hear me callin'?" he said.

It was David who told the ex-con to put up the fence. He had
seen him walk through a crowd of tired men at the woodyard and
balance a rolling log with his foot; the ex-con would say something to it and it would take, the log would take to the foot and be
still. David Harris had discovered an absence in the ex-con, shared
an invisible loneliness with him. But it was not solitude that caused

David to invite him. He wanted to stick out his foot and stop light, point to something and tell it to hush, make everything in the world dark again.

It could have been a secret were it not for the vein that leaped up and grabbed him, causing him to think.

It was evident to the ex-con, while looking at David's swollen face, the closed eye of his masked skin, that a fever was riding him. He had seen the wasps swarming around him, the mood of unprotection belittling him.

"I'm coming," said Too.

You would have thought that David would have heard this voice of magnetism and walked away. But he did not. He stood there watching her, the strict confinement of her feet on the ground, the loose talk between the woman he had married and the man he had invited.

The ex-con shook hands with Too as she disappeared through the back door of the house, holding David by the ribs, as if she had been called by a spoiled child to help this man to bed.

The ex-con saw Logic in the window. She was holding a paring knife, her arms hanging down beside her. She was turned to the side, her stomach rising as she breathed. He wondered how old she was, what position she took when confronted by ordinary troubles. She was not common. This, he knew. He had seen his mother stand as this little girl. It was the moment she realized that her husband had been cheating on her with a wide-lipped girl from Alabama. It was the moment she poured out the medicine, the bottles of pills he had been using to ease the pain in his liver, and replaced them with aspirin. Aspirin was bad for the body. A woman who gave her husband crushed aspirin in those days, to coat a disease, was out to kill him. And kill him she did, before burying him next to a slaughterhouse.

Logic felt him staring through the window and vanished. She had carved the first word on her stomach: *I*.

Night had come. Logic had earned her ten cents from the Missis and was out on the porch when the man-made-of-paper pulled up in George's yard again. He opened the door of his car, his hands moving. The children were asleep: George appeared under the hanging lantern on the porch.

She looked at the man-made-of-paper's silhouette. He opened his arms to her and hissed. But she did not move. She pulled up her gown and sat down on the steps of her house. The man-made-of-paper joined her.

At first, she was strict. You could only hear the man-made-of-paper mumbling. He grabbed her around the waist and laughed.

She hushed him: the children were sleeping.

The man-made-of-paper pulled her toward him.

She turned away.

He pulled harder, until she slapped him.

He held the side of his face, looking at George, whose hair was a page of static.

"Who else is gonna show you love?" he asked loudly.

George paid him no mind: his voice had startled the universe.

Calmly, without any hesitation, she answered him, "My children."

She wished she could have told him what it was, how abruptly she rose from the table in her house and felt her pounding heart rise through her gown—she swore that had she swallowed, she would have fallen onto the floor. Perhaps she would have, if she had not imagined how silly her hand would have looked with no one to place it perfectly beside her.

logic

The man-made-of-paper walked away from the steps. There was no thinking about it. He opened the door of his car and left the prostitute's house. He went in a hurry too. He knew that, had he stayed much longer, the whore would be dead.

George. George did not move. Not in the beginning.

But then she started for the door. No, she was not ready to go inside. She felt the company of someone watching her tonight.

She was not alone.

Perhaps, it was the unbound gravity of her face that caused George to walk across the road to where Logic lay on the front porch of her house, her eyes closed in an effort to create her own midnight.

This is when Logic felt the lips of a woman kissing her before walking away, back to the broken house, the tracks of dust where the man-made-of-paper's face was somewhere burning.

chapter
eighteen

Logic picked up a creature under the oak tree and the tallest told her to put it down before she got ringworms. She watched it crawl up her arm, tickling her. Then, she looked up at the tallest, who was sitting with his back against the tree trunk, and put it back where she'd found it.

The tallest's hands were still dampened by his mother's bath-water. She had called him from his room to lye her down. He could feel the dirt from the men being washed away. Usually, she spoke to him about one thing or another. But this morning, she was quiet. He wondered if it was cramps that made her so or the long list of stones that she had found in her kidneys.

He had heard the old woman say, in the activity of her dreams, that it was not stones George had found but jealous wives in high-heeled shoes trampling her intestines.

"Where your mama?" asked Logic.

The tallest pulled her hair to see if it was artificial and answered, "She gone to the doctor."

"The doctor?" repeated Logic.

"Yeah," said the tallest. "She got presidents inside her."

"Presidents?"

"Yeah," said the tallest, "presidents."

"Like who?"

The tallest rubbed his nose and looked up the tree. "Like Abe Lincolns."

"Abe Lincolns?"

"They got caught up yonder," said the tallest, pointing to his belly, downward.

"How they get caught up yonder?"

"They was elected," said the tallest. "The world put 'em in office."

"What kind o' office?"

"The kidney," he said. "You ever seen the kidney on a body map?"

"No," said Logic.

"It's velvet," said the tallest. "Like the fancy stuff."

"Fancy?"

"Yeah," said the tallest, "and the men come into the office without wiping they feet, and the next thing you know it's static in the kidney room."

"Static?"

"Uh-huh," said the tallest, "static. Like electricity or something. That's why my mama so magnetic. She real magnetic. Now she's got the Abe Lincolns, 'cause the men didn't wipe they feet."

"Oh," said Logic.

Of all things possible to disturb them, they heard it, a noise that came from the Missis' house that would have been important had it not sounded, from the beginning, that it wanted to be left alone. It was the tallest who found her out in front of her house. Dead. And dragged her white behind up the flight of stairs, gave her life.

He wouldn't have thought about it now, had she not guaranteed it.

It was awful, downright malicious, what she made him do.

"You ever been kissed before?" Now the tallest was asking the questions. His double-jointed arms were in the air; he was chasing blowflies away.

Logic heard her father's voice in her ears: If you ever tell, I will take Celesta to the woodyard and chop her up. But nonetheless, she answered the tallest. "Yeah."

"Where 'bout?" asked the tallest.

She pointed to her head. This was where her father liked to be kissed . . . in his head.

The position of her body, while answering the question posed to her, caused the tallest's shoulders to tremble.

"You long gone," he said. "'Ain't you got any power left?'"

Logic shrugged her shoulders.

"You done let your power get dark," he said.

Logic shrugged her shoulders again, this time as if to say she didn't care.

"You got Job in there now," he said.

This struck a nerve in Logic. "But he didn't mind light in 'im."

The tallest lay beside her. "Yeah," he said, "a man don't ask for light till the end." He picked up a rock and put it inside her hands. "Like this . . . feel."

The rock was no star. It was solid, solid like problems and mathematicians who could tell the difference between a trapezoid and the insanity of numbers. "What's it called?" asked Logic.

"The inferno."

"This where presidents go?" asked Logic.

"Some o' 'em," said the tallest.

"Like Abe Lincolns?" asked Logic, who had turned the questions around again.

"Like men."

"How they get out?" asked Logic.

"We gotta pray for 'em," said the tallest. "We still got static on our shoes."

"Oh."

The tallest was amazed at how a silver coin had fallen from his pocket and made no sound. It lay there on the ground, the tail side showing, before he retrieved it.

When night arrived, David was in the kitchen eating the rabbit he had killed. Too had prepared it with tea bags she had gotten from the Missis.

"What you put in here?" asked David.

"Tea," said Too, sitting down beside him.

David pushed the plate away from him. "I can't eat no more," he said. "It's ruint."

He walked to his bedroom and stood on the boards. The metal loop atop the house was whistling in the curves of the wind. He had thought, many times, of pulling it out of the rectangular wood, but he did not have time.

"Logic!" yelled Too.

She wanted someone to eat the rabbit. She had been in the kitchen all day sautéing the meat and putting lemon in the base to remove the scent of the bullet that had killed it. Surely, Logic would eat it—for she had a peculiar sense of taste, although she did not know what it was.

Logic showed up in the nightgown that Too had laid out for her.

The rabbit was lying on its side. The porcelain plate was covered in long-stemmed yard onions.

"Eat," said Too, pushing the food in front of Logic.

Eat girl.

Eat.

Logic could not remember the last drop of food that had gone into her mouth. And why would she? No one ever called her to eat or noticed the thinning of her hands, the bones like a skeleton trying to breathe.

"Go on," whispered Too, returning to the stove, "Eat."

"Okay," she said, but she wanted to say that if girls could eat when they wanted to, eat without vomiting it all up, without vomiting up the world, that she'd sit here in this chair in this kitchen and . . . it takes a brave girl to swallow hunger, especially now, when her belly is so private that its got no choice but to turn it down.

When Logic bit down on the meat, she felt the rising vomit in her intestines. Her mother, there in front of the stove, was blurry now. The light of the candle in the window was blinding. Her head was false. She was made of wine or whiskey. Or bait.

Too raised her hands in midair, but she did not hold onto Logic. Perhaps she thought she could stop her from falling apart. But she did not want to. She turned away, as if she had not witnessed the imbalance of the world around her.

"Mama," said Logic.

Too, still turned, heard these words and wanted so badly to catch Logic. She had hoped, after stitching her head up, that this would be the first word to come out of her. But it was not. Too had detached herself from this open-minded child, as she did when she threw a placenta into the hollow space of a wastebasket.

Nothing convinced her to turn around.

Logic was on the floor now, lying in a pool of water and rabbit.

chapter
nineteen

The lamb: she saw it.

There where it was called for and struck a heavy blow.

The head open, the mouth vertical.

She heard the sound of a man calling another, a long word, a long death breathing nakedly behind the blood where the red was turning sharp.

chapter
twenty

Run and tell somebody.
    Run and tell.
    Tell somebody.

chapter
twenty-one

Logic had used her finger to call the tallest to her.

She was on the steps of her house with her legs closed, the sky growing dark; the world had become trapped by shadows, the trees moving though the force of wind, as if it had just been pushed from the hips of the earth.

The tallest said he'd stay just a little while. His head was hurting and he had felt something rising within his narrow body. His face was hidden, his fingers separated, the one eye showing, the tip of the nose exposed.

"What dead mean?" asked Logic.

She looked at him, listening to the sound of his breath running forward.

"Dead mean your head don't turn no more," he said.

"Your head don't turn no more?" asked Logic.

"No," he said, one hand coming down from the face, "and your eyes be closed and your heart be still . . . and your heart be still. . . ." He wanted to say more, but the sound of his temples made a noise that could not be silenced.

Eventually, it stopped and he kept on. He kept on about the

body, how it shut down and how the bowels moved and how the bones turned to dust.

"And your head don't turn and your eyes be closed?" asked Logic.

"Yeah," said the tallest, both hands down from the face, "and the presidents keep on till they catch up with something quiet, so they can aggravate it, make it shout."

"Shout?"

"Uh-huh," said the tallest.

"What they do that for?"

"'Cause they need something to open their mouths to, make cold," said the tallest.

"Somebody ever make your cold shout?"

"No," said the tallest.

"What you gone do when somebody make your cold shout?"

The tallest paused. "You won't know when your cold shout," he said. "When the Abe Lincolns come, you'll go and you won't know why you'll go, but you will and you'll lay your head down till you know nothing else of the world."

He hid his face again. "But I ain't wurr'd none."

"Why not?" asked Logic.

The tallest stood up, his temple throbbing again: "Because He already happened, and He is happening again."

chapter
twenty-two

The old woman's hand was still dripping.

She was in no order there on the porch of the house, her wet hand unchanged, as does a reflexive eye: a stranger would blink if he saw her shadow on the ground, slinging the hand away from her body as if she were trying to shake the bones out on purpose.

curtis brought the baby out of the house; he wanted to drop it. He looked down at the object; he could do it if he wanted, go out to the very end of the porch and pretend, like boys do, that he was tired.

A straight line is dangerous when it is crooked.

curtis could speak now.

He could drop this baby on the ground and crack this egg in two.

He could say, I am not quiet. And if you come one step closer, you'll regret it. I swear.

My mother is alive, he'd say.

And I am the boy who will crack this egg in two.

The baby began to cry; the old woman took it out of his arms.

Her hand no longer wet but dry.

* * *

The girl was holding a screwdriver.

"Put that thing up," said the old woman. "You gone put some-body's eye out."

The girl ran into the house and came back empty-handed. The tallest did not look at her. He had been out on the steps all morn-ing, telling visitors that his mama had the Abe Lincolns. Each of the men looked to the old woman for an answer, but she was not concerned.

The baby began to cry again. She sent curtis into the house for a nose pump. When he returned, she pushed the tube up the baby's nose and wiped the mucus on her shirt. Then everyone heard the familiar engine coming up the road: it was the man-made-of-paper.

He was dressed in a vanilla oxford and trousers. curtis looked at the baby, then at the man-made-of-paper. He pointed to his lips and compared them to the infant's. When the old woman looked at him, he whispered something in her ear.

"Nice piece o' wind we got today," said the man-made-of-paper.

The old woman patted the baby on the back. The man-made-of-paper had not seen him since birth. "George gone," she said.

The tallest had spent the entire morning turning cars and men around. But it was this man he could not open his mouth to. He leaned against the wooden column and smiled when he saw Logic on her porch rocking Celesta to sleep.

"Where she headed off to?" asked the man-made-of-paper.

"Surgery," said the old woman.

The man made of paper looked through the open door of the house, as if he had been told that prostitutes could not get sick. "Surgery?" he asked. "Some'n gone bad on 'er?"

A fly buzzed around the baby's bottom.

The old woman did not answer him.

"Now," said the man-made-of-paper, "if some'n gone bad on 'er I got a right to know. She is a common—"

The old woman interrupted him. "Like you is common," she said. "Like all o' us is common."

"I got a wife," said the man-made-of-paper.

"So what I'm s'posed to do?"

"Tell me if she got the shakes," he said.

The old woman sat up from the rocking chair and started for the house. She could turn her back on his kind. A woman who knows where she's going doesn't need to be afraid of ghosts. But for babies, there was nothing merciful about her. Not anymore.

The man-made-of-paper looked down at the tallest: "What your Mo got, son?"

The tallest reached down into his pocket and gave him a penny, his mind in a place of boys, dresses.

Logic was in her room, filling out a birth certificate for Celesta.

PLACE OF BIRTH: Birds.

TIME OF BIRTH: 3:14 P.M.

CITY: Celesta (girls are their own cities)

STATE: Ms (and their own states)

ZIP CODE: All sevns.

BIRTH MOTHER'S MAIDEN NAME: Logic

NAME OF THE BIRTH FATHER: Pa

She looked at the red ink on the page; it was catastrophic. She suddenly began to feel sick. It was not food at all that had exploded in her mouth; it was red ink.

She ran to the mirror and looked at her tongue. She saw red. She had been holding the pen in her mouth between letters and could feel the gradual pull, the odor of gravity. She started to scream. David, his face gone down, and Too appeared in the door.

"Lawd Jesus," said Too, "what you done did now?"

Logic pointed to the writing pen, her tongue collapsed, a smooth muscle.

"Well, don't sit up there and swallow it," said David. "Rinse your mouth out!"

She ran to the water basin in the backyard and began gulping the water down. She felt the redness inside of her. It was coating her tubes. Her first thought was that the butterflies were becoming infected. She rinsed and rinsed and rinsed, until the feeling left her.

She had a lot of praying to do.

Immediately, she ran back to her room and blew the lantern out. She began to speak to the Ultimate One. In her own words:

In His will is my peace.
In His will is my peace.

David was getting out of his clothes. He looked down at the sheets, at the birth certificate he had picked up from Logic's bedroom. Too was shutting the doors of the house when he struck a match to the paper: the red ink began to wither away in flames. Blue. Yellow. Orange. Gone.

Too smelled the burning from the kitchen. "David?"

He did not respond.

"What's burning?"

Under his breath, he whispered an answer that belonged to God.

Logic was on the other side of the wall. She was no longer on her knees but standing next to the window, her hand pressed against the glass, where she was sure she had heard the voice of the ex-con, humming alongside her in prayer.

chapter
twenty-three

It was July in Valsin County, Mississippi. The Missis had given Logic a silver bank to keep her dimes in. It was a flat box. The four corners were the color of cigar smoke. And there was a little lady, dressed in pink, who spun around when she opened it. At her slippers was a slit in which to bury her coins. She hid it under the feathers of her mattress, alive.

The ex-con was in the backyard. He seemed to have overslept. The residue of a man dreaming was in his eyes, and he did not hide it from even the tiniest stranger. There, on the outside, he was hauling a load of wood behind him. He had aligned them, one by one, on the acre of land he was to separate. The flies were like falling snow around him: the whiteness of northern pictures, the sleigh on the roof of a chimney.

He began to dig up the earth. A hole here. A hole a few feet away. His stomach started to rumble. It was the nostalgic glance of The Principle, the man of all men, who had taken him apart. He was constantly lying on his bunk with a shank in his hand. Wherever he was, he was lying, whether standing or drinking from a well of tears in his dreams. He was holding the shank and waiting for The Principle in the lower bunk to wake him. He could hear the sound of the toilet running, the constant train coming down the tracks of the sewerage. It was coming for him. He waited for it to arrive each night but had fallen asleep waiting. Yes, a man falls asleep waiting on what he cannot have.

Every sound was important. He learned to recognize when things mattered. He slept with the picture of his daughter, Pilot, in his hands. She was his only protection. She made him feel like a man: the tiny bird in her throat, the innocence of her fallen hand when sleeping. She had matched him perfectly. There were no tidal waves to crush her from below. Because he had protected her. He had shown her the protection of the mothers and grandmothers and aunts who had raised him. He had many, many mothers. They had taught him how to lay his words down.

But he carried a pulsating memory within him. Once, as a boy, he had begun to hang with a gang from the city, boys with games and lyrics enough to kill Goliath in the dead of summer. He had found himself behind the house of an old man, blind and deaf. He and the gang had looked in on him many nights: the way he tapped the palm of his daughter's hand, the calmness of his outstretched arms when wanting to be nude. They had seen him, studied him for months before waiting for the women to leave the house: the old woman with a cracked tooth and the daughter she never looked upon, touched. The gang had put him up to it, because he had nervousness within him. If he was to be a good thief, diligent, he was to take.

He remembered being pushed through the back door of the old man's house. But once inside, he could not do it. He had heard, when a child, that the deaf and blind were angels. Please, they'd say, leave the angels alone.

What he did manage to pull from the shelf of many books was the life of an Italian philosopher. He hid the spine under his sweater, cold at the ribs. When he heard the old man stirring, he ran out of the house, ran with a bellyful of words that would later turn into prayers.

He wished he could admit that this was the last time he had stolen something. But he could not. Much later, he had befriended a woman who did not know how to use a gun. He loved her; she had a hidden education. She had come from a family of illiteracy and had learned her own language. A white woman had taught her how to speak Italian; she, in turn, taught him. And they, at night, took turns reading the philosopher's words. She was made of magic. And Pilot, the child she brought into the world, was also made of magic. She was a curious child. Even at birth, she was equipped with light. So he put lightning bugs around her to watch her eyes burn. She was Christ to him. But even Christ could not bring the totality of restraint to the world.

The ex-con took a job in the city and began to visit the woman and Pilot on weekends. One particular evening, he noticed that her ring had been stolen, the promise ring he had given her before Pilot was born. Someone had broken into the house.

He was outraged and traveled back to the city on hate alone. He looked in on the owner of a pawnshop. He had asked him days before how much he could get a .22 for. Although the price was cheap, he still could not afford it on his salary; he worked for waste management. But he had heard the pawnbroker speak of his heart, the bad blood in it. So he robbed the place, his index finger under his shirt; left the old man with his mouth open, his hand over his chest; and returned to Pilot and the woman.

He loaded the gun.

But he did not show the woman how to use it.

It was in her hands when it exploded: a surge of fire, like lightning, trapped in her head.

Before long, the metal doors closed behind him; he was in the stone jungle, and The Principle was offering him a pack of cigarettes. He wished now that he had never taken them. What a man pays in prison for smokes!

He had gotten his uniform and rubbed his fingers across the numbers. He moved when the voices told him to move. He showered when the voices told him to. He lived in a system of parasites. You were damaged when you walked the concrete. And God could not stop The Principle from penetrating you. God is in your mind when in prison. You pray and pray and pray and blame everything on the devil to keep the buzzards from gouging your eyes out. You take stitches in places that are too subhuman for body maps even. You are an animal. And you will be locked up with the others as an animal, whether you are innocent or not.

All the first-timers were bunked with The Principle. He knew how to get past the guards, how to get brothers a piece of lead pipe in the jungle. He *was* the system. And the system always obliges the dangerous ones. Because it is the dangerous ones who know the game.

The first night was a motherfucker. The ex-con lay on his bunk thinking of brain matter, death, Pilot in the lap of the state. He heard The Principle calling out to the others. He was made of Styrofoam or rubber; something without feelings. His teeth had been sharpened, the canines fit to keep V-shaped blades hidden.

The ex-con had heard of prison: the horror stories of men turned transvestites, feathers. But he had heard the green side of things too: Get in good with the heathens on the yard. The heathens will protect you. Naïveté kills in the jungle.

Lights out.

And there he was on the cot, lying with his face turned to the wall, when The Principle grabbed him from behind. He thought he had fought men, that he could fight any man. But he was unprepared. The Principle had spent almost twenty years in the jungle. He was the first out on the yard, weights in hand, lifting the pounds of metal above his thick shoulders; there was a large serpent tattooed on his forearm.

It was the longest night of the ex-con's life.

"Go away," he whispered. To the memory, the penetration.

He had put two logs in the holes behind Logic's house now. He was relieved by the old woman's singing. She discovered a deep contraction inside of him. Everything was shortened. Every feeling released on the wrong side of his anatomy. It had taken him many years to feel. The jungle had left him with the seeds of numbness. The old woman hummed:

> *Hope me.*
> *Somebody hope me.*

He had become radiant inside. Just a touch. He would work himself out of The Principle. He would work for free, until he could hear the roaring of the train coming for him. Perhaps he would not fall asleep. Perhaps it was only in his head.

chapter
twenty-four

Logic was asleep.

Too lay in bed, her face turned, her index finger pressed on the cheek where she had begun to tap lightly on the bone; she had been there for hours, trying to describe it, to find a word to match the feeling of a woman waiting . . . waiting for what she could neither balance nor protect.

The door opened. She could smell David, feel him coming toward her. Perhaps, she thought, the air beneath the covers would rise upward, like the blood that had caused the odor of his mother's body to find his crying at birth, bring him to her fully.

She hoped he would lift the linen, bring his hand to her thigh, go to the center of her life where life, indeed, came from. Touch it. Bring his clothes down in the moonlight, penis erect, so she could bring it forward, sit on top of it. Her breasts bare. Her mouth open, wide.

But she could feel the danger around her, his hand, as a man's does at a moment when he cannot identify who and what he is, striking her face in darkness. Her face going down, forced against the linen, her life out in the open, the odor of her vagina muted.

But force she had felt and force she did not care about.

For she did not know what time it was in her own body, although right now, at this moment, her body was in the midnight position, striking loudly against a hollow object.

Inanimate.

David walked through the door, and she pulled the linen away from her thighs. If he would not insist upon it, upon taking her, she would leave the valves in her body open to plea and judgment. She reached for him in the darkness but could only see his eye moving away.

He sighed.

She moved for a moment, but her movement was not concentrated upon. She was not aware of it. She found herself standing before him, bringing his fingers to her body; she wanted to say please.

And then she felt his penis.

It was not erect.

He pushed her away.

It was now, in darkness, that he realized why he could not reach out his foot and stop light. Oh, it shook him. He was so cold. He could not think. He hoped it was not true. It was out in front of him, the finger that had gone down his throat and caused him to cry.

Go away, he whispered.

Too was not certain, but she thought she heard him say, *I can't breathe.*

chapter
twenty-five

Lightning had struck a fragile tree alongside the Missis' house, and were it not for Too, lying in the dismal room, she would have run down to the little garden in front of her house and peed in it. To think of it now, how delirious she was before Too's coming, made her seem all the more accessible to the darkness around her.

Logic was good and wet now.

She had known better than to stand out in the rain, when the climate was so unpredictable that it could have taken an enormous breath and blown her to pieces.

David was on the other side of the wall; he became sick with the pattern of breathing, the prayers coming from Logic's lungs. The language that came from her: the low levels of whispering, the winding of some strange object. And the music. Why couldn't he have stopped the music? It was unsafe to be in her company. It was unsafe to be alive, on this side of the wall, with this child praying to the same God whom he had prayed to while walking to the woodyard.

His nightmares were closer to flesh than images. Logic's brain was open—like the intestines of a beast. And he, he was as minute

as a hair on her head. The jackhammer was in his hands. He plowed
the opening up; he saw the hidden words of her prayers. He could
not speak them—for he saw a man who looked like Moses or God
standing on the edge of a verb, daring him.

He touched the open cavity in his wisdoms. It was dark, and
there was a throbbing pain going up the side of his face; the tooth
was rotting. He held his jaw and turned over on the pillows. Yes,
it was the Johnsons he had smelled. Too had not washed her hands
after coming. He saw it, a giant seahorse floating toward him. The
eye partially hidden beneath the lid. Open and dark.

Yes, thank goodness, it was all being pushed into the lake by
now, like a radio.

Or prostitute.

Logic began to speak to Celesta. She wondered if she was cold,
if she was in the mood for talking. Celesta answered her. And she
told her to keep her mouth closed.

David was not aware that the sky had lit up. He was stuffing
the tobacco back inside his jaw. On his hand was a cut from the
barbwire; the ex-con was looking him in the eye while talking and
he had grown nervous, off balance, stopping his fall on the razor-
sharp edges of the barbwire. He showed no pain and the ex-con
pretended not to notice. And now, with the skin of his fingers
turned upward, he wondered how he would grab hold of the logs
in the morning.

He was drifting away, almost entirely asleep, when he saw
Celesta's leg being dragged before him in the open door. She was
not human, he thought. She had no voice like Logic or bones. She
was mute.

"Logic?" he asked.

He was afraid, although there was no saying so. There were times when he could not fight the names: the faggots or the sissies. Like now.

Logic had not answered him for some time. He got up and walked toward the door. The grasshoppers were making music. The storm had passed. He turned and looked out the window. And turned back, before seeing Celesta's arm disappear into Logic's room.

This was a danger to him, having these silent footsteps in the house. He'd heard that the mind deceived itself in darkness, but he had thought himself into obscurity. He was losing his sanity. "Logic?"

Finally, she answered him. "Yes, sir."

He waited a moment; she was moving around again.

Celesta was back in the corner. Logic slid underneath the covers.

David felt the tobacco settling in his stomach. "What does it mean?" he asked.

She was fully awake, her eyes open in the darkness like her mother's.

David lay on the pillows again. Perhaps she had not heard him ask. He put his face up to the wall, the cavity roaring like a dark train; he whispered, "What does it all mean?"

Logic put her fingers up to where she thought his mouth was, closed it.

chapter
twenty-six

The arc in Logic's stomach was beginning to rise. She felt something moving around in there. The butterflies were growing up. They were making her sleepy, terribly dizzy. She looked around the house for tall objects to stick inside of her. She wanted to open herself up and let the butterflies out.

How desperate she was; she had never been so desperate in her entire life.

She had thought of igniting the pituitary gland of the tallest. It was paper. And she wanted to create fire. Not this, she thought, but something else. If she had spread her legs open wide enough, the butterflies would come to the light and she could set them free.

Or music. Perhaps, if she reached for the silver dime box with the dancing ballerina, the butterflies would stop fluttering for a moment and fly out of her stomach. But no. Not music.

Something else.

Something else.

It was not so much that she was desperate to let them go as it was the condition they had put her in. She sat on her bed and thought about the things of the world and how they were made, if they could fit into her vagina and not cut up her abdomen coming out: a butter knife, a teaspoon.

She looked at the pituitary gland and saw the shape of the intestines. She must have known, all the while, that it lay in her very own closet: one of the hangers that her mother had told her to put down.

She picked it up and lay back.

She had not yet taken off her panties when she heard a knock at the door.

The iron hanger was under her pillow now.

She turned the knob; it was the ex-con. He had formed an Amen with his hands, one on top of the other.

"Logic?" he said.

She nodded.

The items of his face were aligned like a column. "I caught this light the other night," he said. "Been saving it up for you ever since."

He signaled for her to look through the tiny cracks of his fingers; there were lightning bugs in there.

Logic turned and listened to the empty house. There was no safety in her own body. So nothing on the outside was dangerous: "Put 'em in there," she said, pointing to the operating room; it could not be seen from where he stood, but he walked behind her slowly.

"I figured they'd be dead by now," he said. "Light don't last long, you know."

So he laughed. But it was the laughter of nervousness. He stood in this place where the operations were, the penetrations, and looked down on the table from where Logic had witnessed the lighted candle; it had quickly, distinctly, gone out.

The ex-con had gotten away from The Principle, he thought. The Principle was still locked up in the penitentiary; there was no way he had gotten past the buzzers. He could smell him in this room: his crotch, the semen coming out of his penis. In this room, he was back on the cell block, getting fucked by The Principle and his boys.

He opened his hands and looked down at Logic. She was as innocent as Pilot, standing there. He could even hear the tiny bird in her voice too.

The lightning bugs were hovering over them.

"You gotta leave now, mister," she said.

He sighed and walked out the back door where his work awaited him, as he began to look at his hands, up at God.

Logic had gone to ring the bell and was on her way home when the tallest jumped out in front of her. "Scat!" he shouted.

Logic didn't blink at all. She had been holding her belly and had come up with another idea. She grabbed the tallest and ran around the side of her house. Her bedroom window was open; she reached down until her fingers landed on the brown paper bag. Her materials were in there: the hanger, the cotton swabs, the leech, the fishing twine.

She signaled for the tallest to hush.

"Well," he said, "I gotta pee. What you want me to do, sit here 'n' pee on myself?"

He walked over to the holes that the ex-con had made and peed in one of them, whispering. "Good Lawd," he said, "I thought my peter was gone bust op'n!"

The moon was split open above them. Logic could hear her folks in the kitchen. Too was talking about the Missis and all that money she was giving her to ring the bell. And, of course, David was sitting in silence.

Logic grabbed the tallest's hand and whispered something in his ear; he opened the brown paper bag. He had seen these tools before when his mother couldn't afford to let her belly swell up.

He jumped down off the table and told her to wait a second. He went running around the corner of her house. She heard him run up the front steps of his porch and slam the door. The old woman started to holler. He had woken the baby up.

Logic was on her hands and knees. She could hear her father asking Too where she was; "She went to ring the bell," she said.

"But it done rung, Too."

"Ain't nothin' grabbed her," said Too. "Just her and the Missis up there makin' angels, that's all."

"Makin' angels?" asked David.

"Yeah," said Too. "Even got the lamb to go wit' it."

David grew silent again.

When he pushed his chair back, Logic heard the tallest starting for her house again. The door slammed back and he yelled, "Good Lord!"

The old woman shouted back at him, "I'm gone Good Lord you, you keep that racket up!"

The tallest shouted, as if under a glass jar, "Yes, ma'am!"

By the time he made it around the corner, David was in his bedroom window with his hands on the wall. The lightning bugs were flying upward. They had gotten used to the space in the operating room.

"Shhhh," said Logic.

The tallest returned with a lantern, grabbing her hand. They went flying past the large oak tree, along the path where Logic had discovered North Dakota, and there, where the crickets yelled, he stopped for a moment to catch his breath. "We better slow down 'fore my head start hurtin'."

He put the lantern on the ground and shook the matches in his pocket, pulling them out. He struck one on the side of the box and when the oxygen caught it, lit the wick. Logic was beside him, breathing heavily.

"Looka yonder," he said, pointing to a wild rabbit that scurried through the woods. He then touched Logic's face. "You scared?"

Logic looked around her, up at the moon. "Uh-uh."

The tallest had a name for where she stood, called it the circus-of-me.

He grabbed her by the arm again. "We gotta get goin'!"

They had come to a clear patch of earth between the trees. He pointed for Logic to lie down on the grass. "You got panties on?" he asked.

Logic nodded.

"Well," he said, "take 'em off. And don't worry 'bout me seeing you none. 'Cause I ain't doing no North Dakotas tonight."

She pulled the panties over her ankles.

The tallest emptied the materials into his shirt and flattened the brown paper bag. Once he did this, he put the materials down on it, like doctors do in surgery. "All right now," he said. "Let's pray."

Logic started to get up.

"No," he said, "stay there. I'm gone pray for both o' us."

He put his hands together, as had the ex-con when he had trapped the lightning bugs in his fingers. "Lord," said the tallest, "I'm fixin' to fix her. And please, don't let me run into no Abe Lincolns while I'm down under. Amen and Amen." He looked at Logic and made her spit on his hand. "Promise never to tell!" he yelled.

"All right," said Logic. "I promise."

"I could get sent up north for this here," said the tallest. "And I ain't gettin' my hands dirty mendin' fences, either. Understand?"

Logic nodded.

"Now," said the tallest. "Open up!"

In the beginning, Logic tightly clenched her legs shut. The tallest gave her the eye and she opened them a little. "Wider," said the tallest. "Wider . . . okay."

He put the lantern up to her legs and opened her vagina. He tried first with his finger to reach the butterflies, but Logic was making noises. He reached on the ground for a stick. "Here," he said, "when it gets to hurtin', bite down on that."

He couldn't see her face, only the bone of her chin shivering.

The lips were open and he stuck his finger back in her vagina. He thought he felt something at first. But then, nothing. "How long them thangs been up there?" he asked.

Logic showed him a sign of the fingers: three.

He bent the hanger so it would be upright and told her to bite down on the stick. He took the curved end and opened the lips of her vagina, getting it inside of her partially. She started to scream. But he kept going until the full curve had disappeared. He turned it sideways and pulled it out. There was no blood on it or butterflies.

And then he began to think of George, his mother: the night the man came to her house and did this to her, she almost bled to death. He had gone to lay her back down and saw her lying fetally, her body underwater. And remembered the pain that went through her, how it was impossible for him to reach her from behind. She had turned dark and could only lie in her bed in blood, the sheets filling up in a pile in the corner of the room.

Logic looked at him, as if silently asking if he had pulled them out.

He shook his head and had begun to dip the cotton swabs in the alcohol to clean the tip of the hanger. This was when he realized that he had scraped her somewhere. He saw blood.

It frightened him. He stood up over this girl, Logic, who had learned in no time where North Dakota was located. She could be saved, but not by him. She was not made of plastic or bullies or New Orleans. She was not retarded because she had fallen out of the sky.

He turned away from her.

He could not do it.

He was not the man. The man came to his house and laid his mother down on her bed, her legs up. And stuck the hanger in her belly and pulled out a fetus. He had stuck many hangers up the bellies of women, because he was the man. The man is not the woman. And the man cannot feel what is not within him to save.

It was no secret that he knew he was not looking for butterflies.

"Put your panties on," he said.

Logic's eyes were filled with tears. She had really believed that the thumping in her ribs, the spirit of activity, was what had caused her to levitate. She could not remember climbing the tree and sitting on the branch. Her body was filled with cold things, like floating semen with wings.

She sat up and looked at the tallest, who was standing away from the lantern so she could not see his tears come down, then at the hanger that was lying lifelessly on the ground. She stood up over the lantern with her legs open, hoping the butterflies would see the light and fly away. But nothing: only the kerosene whistling.

She put her panties on and felt something coming from her down-below, dripping on the ground beneath her. She touched her inner thigh with her hand and when it returned to her eyes, it was filled with the light touch of blood.

The tallest reassured her: "It'll go away," he said. "I didn't go far up enough to scar you. But you'll be sore tomorrow."

"Sore?" she asked.

"Yeah," he said, "put some salt in your bathwater to dry up the scratch."

They abandoned the brown paper bag in the woods. He held onto her every step of the way, as if he had been holding his life in his hands.

"The butterflies," said Logic. "Are they still in me?"

The tallest turned away. He had blown the wick out, sighing: "Yeah," he said, "they still in you."

But it was not happening to her.

It was happening to Celesta.

chapter
twenty-seven

Run and tell who?
    Who I run and tell?

chapter
twenty-eight

Two weeks passed.

Logic was in her bed when she heard the tallest tap softly on the window. He had roused her out of a deep sleep. She wiped her eyes and looked at him, his large forehead resting on the glass, and opened the window.

He shook her. "Logic," he whispered, "wake up. Logic."

She opened her eyes widely.

When he realized that he had gotten her attention, he sighed. "I had a dream," he said.

She mumbled.

"Logic," he said, shaking her again. "You hear me? Wake up 'fore the ol' man get going."

She was fully up now.

"My mama done went off 'n' joined the army," he said.

Logic stared at him strangely. "The army?"

"Yeah," he said. "She had on a uniform and stuff. Like a soldier or some'n other."

He paused. "She wadn't fighting none. . . . Wadn't in no hurry neither."

"What she was doing, then?" asked Logic.

"Flyin'," he said.

"For real?" whispered Logic. "Like a bird?"

"Yeah," he said, "like a bird. Didn't even have the Abe Lincolns." He folded his arms and smiled. "Now, go figger."

The chain on the metal loop began to cry. She looked at the tallest and pushed his head down. She could hear her father on the other side of the wall, mumbling. The chain was quiet for a moment; then the chiming picked back up.

"You better scat," she whispered.

She could see the shadow of the tallest's forehead on the ground, the bones protruding. He crawled around the side of the house and disappeared, something howling in the darkness behind him.

His mother had not gone to the army.

Her head would no longer turn.

Her heart was still.

She was dead.

The old woman was sitting on her porch mourning George's death when a preacher from Pyke County pulled up in the yard. The gossip had landed throughout Mississippi, and the question seemed inevitable: Who was going to bury the prostitute?

The preacher walked up the steps of the house, the same steps where George had sat resisting the man-made-of-paper. He was clean-shaven and walked as if there were lead in his shoes, his face unseen.

The old woman touched his hand and began to scream. "This place ate up wit' evil!" She started to rock, her shoulders moving. "Lawd, help. Help, Lawd. Save these babies; these Valsin babies need saving." She pointed across the road, over toward the Missis' house, where the tree in her yard had muzzled the bell.

The preacher held on to her. Everyone knew, almost a rule in Mississippi, to let the old women get their peaces out. They had held so much in over the years. Because death was something, any woman will tell you, if she is willing to find the words to describe it, that you never get over.

The old woman was hidden behind the preacher's heart; Logic could feel it beating, beating, beating quickly. She was on the porch waiting for the tallest to come out of the house. She looked for him to come running out of the front door, his arms out in front of him.

But he had not, since he heard about his mother's death, moved.

The preacher pulled out a pink handkerchief from his pocket and wiped the old woman's eyes. She held on to this arm, guiding him into the house. She had not stopped screaming; her hand was on her chest, patting the pain that had begun to boil inside of her.

The baby began to cry. He was motherless, as was the tallest, curtis, the girl. Logic could hear the solemn breaks in the baby's cries; the old woman picked him up. She was rocking him now, her hands on his back.

Logic was in the kitchen window, waiting for the hearse to pull up in the tallest's yard. George was to be buried under the large oak tree—where the tallest had climbed up the bark a million times, it seemed, his legs dangling from a high branch.

Logic heard the buzzings of the lightning bugs; no one had been in the operating room since the ex-con let them go. She walked toward the door, opening it. They were concentrated over her body; she pushed the window up and shooed them away.

And they went.

The hearse pulled up in the tallest's yard. The old woman was veiled on the steps, holding the baby. The tallest stood behind her, his eyes swollen; curtis and the girl were shadows. A man in black opened the door of the hearse and put his arms around the old woman's shoulders, the baby silent now.

The tallest looked neither to his sides nor in front of him. He knew the ground where he walked; Mississippi was in his bones. He had cried in the circus-of-me and crept nudely upon the boards of his house. The light in his eyes had been put out: a cloud of deception.

Logic ran up to him. He did not even feel the touch of life; he felt nothing. He had lost the woman who had carried him; she had not cared whether he walked around the house in the nude or whether he wore her red dresses and eye shadow. He did these acts alone, because he wanted to.

George had given him the privilege of choice in his early age; she said nothing when he followed the boys in New Orleans or when he brought home the mannequin with the hole between her legs. She was a prostitute for her children. She had even slept with a man who owned a Ford, just so she could strap the mannequin down to the roof of his car. He remembered now how the plastic woman had gotten home, remembered the roaring of concrete on the highway, the strange signs alongside the road. It was his mother in his system, the love of his life.

A soldier.

A hole had been dug beneath the oak tree. Two men stood beside it from the funeral parlor. The old woman had received help from the church in Pyke County. She'd heard that Jesus lived there. And Logic, when she heard of the struggle the old woman was having to pay for death, emptied her dimes out on her sheets and gave them to her.

The two men opened the hearse and lifted the coffin, wooden. The tallest dropped his eyes and began to sigh deeply. He was now holding the baby. The old woman patted him on the back. Logic stood beside them, her hand on her belly.

The coffin was on a three-belt metal holder. The preacher stood at the head, where there lay an artificial flower, red. The earth is quiet when a prostitute is being buried. There were no men there with Fords or drifters from the county, not even the man-made-of-paper. It could have been, because of men like him, that she had asked the question of love on Too's porch. No one had answered it for her. Not even the shadow on the ground.

The old woman did not know what to tell the tallest about his mother's death, so she told him what she had heard him screaming that day on the steps of the house; she told him the Abe Lincolns busted her kidneys up.

Secrets lie dormant in Mississippi. You never know the full truth about anything. There is what your folks choose to tell you and what you yourself discover. One or the other is poisonous, vain.

The preacher spoke. "Let us bow our heads in prayer."

The old woman began to wince. She was still holding on to the pink handkerchief he had given her, as if it had absorbed all her years of crying.

"Father, Son, and Holy Spirit," said the preacher, "we give this life to You. It is not perfect but human. May You shed mercy upon her soul. Give her the peace of the lamb. The One and Only. In Your Holy name, we pray. Amen."

They all looked up on the branch above them where a sparrow, alive, had begun to sing, as if it had seen many disasters on the back roads of Mississippi.

The preacher stepped back and waited for the two men to lower the body into the ground. The old woman screamed when the coffin landed on the square-plotted dust. She thought of her blind and deaf father, the tapping of his fingers on the palm of her hand when death approached him.

The final words.

The final question: Will it hurt?

She felt him now, the coffin swallowed by the earth.

"George," she whispered. "George. . . . Where you gone to, George?" She looked at the tallest. "Where she done run off to?"

The two men had business to tend to. They picked up the abandoned shovels leaning against the oak tree and began to pack the earth. The old woman fell to her knees; she covered her face with her hands, her mouth, and whispered in the clean summer wind. "You's a soldier now, Georgie. Just like in the war."

Her legs were too stiff to bend in the car. The preacher and one of the two men carried her home. She had fainted.

Logic followed, tapping the fat on her scalp where the dead woman had kissed her.

chapter
twenty-nine

The tallest was in the circus-of-me.

The boy didn't even remember falling asleep.

He thought—he thought he had swallowed a minnow.

The church bells began to ring. Logic was coming down. The leech began to move on her head. She did what she always had to do to remove the feeling: she swallowed.

The Missis was in the kitchen pouring herself a cup of coffee when she walked up behind her. "I'm fix'n to go now," she said.

The Missis turned around and put her white hand delicately behind her neck. "Where you headed?"

There were times when the Missis could not sleep and she'd go walking through the path, under the oak tree, near Logic's window to hear the bird in her belly come alive. She had been this little child, filled with the seeds of the earth, the papas going down inside of her like milk. She had held a killer in her hands before. A killer is something worthy of an adjective. She had stood over the papa, the man, in his sleep with enough bullets in her soul to crystallize him. Like the animals in the hospitals, when a nerve is pinched to sanitize them upstairs. Brave? No, she was not brave.

But one day she would be.

"Bring your friend here," she said. "The boy."

Logic propped her elbows on the table, her hind legs pushing her backside upward. "He don't like the world," she said.

A blade of grass had come into her house. How calm it was, solitary. She could have walked over to it and, with one breath from within, sent it scurrying from its place. But she was aware, so disquiet in her mind, that she knew, almost instantly, that she had to leave it alone.

There broke an intimate noise to disrupt the business of her thinking: a cup had rung like a trembling alarm, rung as if nothing, neither hand nor finger, had caused it to move.

There comes a time when a woman must decide which is more important of the two images in her mind: a cup or a blade of grass.

Not now, please. Not while she is still breathing.

Then there was the magazine in the kitchen window, a woman in uniform, her white teeth strong, perfect. Who could tell, simply by looking, when a woman has been in the operating room? So they saw it, both Logic and the Missis equally, as if never before, the word across the page: seamen.

"I gotta go," whispered Logic.

So she was gone out of the house and when the door slammed, the Missis was unnotified, did not expect it, but it came right out of her nose and shook her entire body: she sneezed.

Logic ran past the oak tree, past George, and looked for a sign of the tallest. She could see his shirt between the bark, his protruding forehead: "Ey," she said.

He turned around and looked at her. There was a faint smile on his face. Life was returning back to him. He put his index finger up to his mouth, signaling for her to stop yelling.

She moved through the bushes and finally flopped down in front of him. "I think my heart done stopped," she said. "All this runnin'!"

"What you tellin' me for?" he said, pointing between the bark. "Whole pond right over yonder."

"That water dirty," said Logic.

The tallest laughed a little. "The water in you dirty," he said. "Don't make no difference."

She looked at his feet, the fine muscle that rode the back of his legs. He was fit to wear his mother's high-heeled shoes. He put his hands together and turned them over repeatedly, as if he was blowing a cotton head from the root.

"My mama wadn't customary, you know," he said.

"Customary?"

"Yeah," he said, "common. Look here." He took off one of the heels and opened a body map that had been taped to the sole. "I figger the Abe Lincolns went up from here"— the vagina—"got caught up in this part"— the fallopian tubes—"started for these"— the bright orange intestines—"and ended up right here"—the kidneys.

Logic put her hands on his eyes and pressed down; she wanted to see if he had been crying still. He pushed her away and she laughed.

He lit up inside for a moment. "I ain't heard you do that in a while."

She laughed again.

He folded the body map up and stuffed it back inside his heels. "Strong as pee when a girl grins, I s'pose."

Logic covered her mouth.

The tallest grew serious, looking across at the pond. "Don't you tell nobody 'bout the circus-o'-me, you hear?"

"Uh-huh," said Logic.

"Spit on it," he said, stretching his hand out to her.

Logic spat on the palm of her hand and shook on it.

"Where that purse?" asked the tallest.

"Home," said Logic. "Under my bed."

"How come you don't wear it no more?"

Logic shrugged her shoulders.

The tallest looked down at his feet. He had dreamed of the blue purse since the first time he laid eyes on it. "Reckon you bring it to the circus-o'-me next time," he said. "You know . . . so I can see if it fit me."

Logic paid him no mind. "The Missis says you're good and welcome."

He did not know the Missis, did not find her dead on the ground or drag her white behind upstairs and put her to bed. There was no trusting her; she was the woman in his dreams.

She was the minnow.

And he was the thing that swallowed her.

The tallest closed his eyes, his arms propped up behind him. "Logic," he said, "anybody ever called you retarded?"

"Retarded?" she asked. "What retarded mean?"

"When you got some'n in your system 'sides sense," he said. "Like slow."

Logic thought about it. "Yeah," she whispered, "somebody called me retarded."

The tallest's eyes filled up with water. There was a well inside of him. He wished he had never asked her, that she had never heard the word. His eyes were open now, up at the orange sun. "Who?" he asked.

"My mama," said Logic.

He raised up on one side of his body. "I'll bet she kept right on breathin' the whole time, didn't she?"

Logic nodded.

The tallest spoke. "The next time somebody calls you retarded—"

He did not speak: he wrote it down in dust.

The tallest couldn't live the rest of his life with the old woman. She had begun to find things in his room, the private parts of who he was. She wanted him to be the way he was in the beginning, a diplomat. But that was before he discovered the circus-of-me, before he had begun to talk to God.

He could never be that same boy again.

Not anymore.

chapter
thirty

David couldn't care less that George was dead. She was just the bitch who lived across the road. His tooth was still bothering him, pulsating. He had thought of taking some pliers and pulling it out, but he was afraid the enamel would crack at the root; the nerve would surely ride him if that happened.

It was noon.

The heat was ripe at this hour.

The ex-con was in the backyard posting the barbwire along the row of logs he had stacked. His job was almost done at the Harrises'. The letter was in his pocket from the state of Mississippi. The government was watching him. Any more trouble and he'd land himself back in the pen with the other numbers, The Principle.

The underlined rule: no gun ownership.

It was good to be back on the earth again, free. Sometimes, he'd wake up in the middle of the night screaming. He still could not shake the nightmares; living in the jungle was a motherfucker for the man. Even when free, he paused before he put the tiniest amount of food in his mouth; he was used to being told when to eat. Used to hiding his balls on the toilet—because there was always some bastard around looking at the size of his dick. Bastards,

turned feathers, who needed the man to penetrate them. He could not lie; he had thought of it. He could close his eyes and think of a virgin, a woman, and bypass the words of the Book, and keep going until the tension ran out of him. He would turn away from the feather, turn away in darkness or a concrete room with pipes.

But he could not.

He wasn't the man.

But he wasn't a sissy either.

David was looking out the window at him. He had not seen Too carry on with him since the day his face was swollen. Where was Logic? he thought. How come he could never find her around the house these days when he needed her? The pain spiraled up to his head; he couldn't take it anymore.

He opened his mouth and grabbed the tooth between two fingers. He jerked hard at the tooth, but nothing. The root was unshakable. He tried again, and the response was like a jackhammer pounding the nerve. He looked in the mirror; the tooth was completely rotten. His gums were beginning to swell. "Dammit!"

Tobacco. He ran for the room and packed the little bit that he had left into the cavity. The pain was not disappearing quickly enough. He went to the kitchen and put a pot of water on the stove; he was going to fill the washbasin in the backyard.

He looked at the gun in the kitchen window. The pain was so disturbing. Had he been drunk, he might've done it. Had Too had the Johnsons and Celesta grown a voice, he would have definitely done it. But not now.

The water began to boil. He could hear the old woman yelling for curtis and the girl to get away from the road; her voice soothed something inside of him. She did not stop the pain completely, but she gave him a voice to listen to, a distraction through the silence. She was beginning to look like his mother.

logic

He could hear curtis running back toward the steps of his house, the girl behind him, asking the old woman if the baby ate this morning. What he could not hear was the rumbling in the old woman's heart. Like the ex-con, she had gotten a letter from the government too. The first had been received while George was alive, warning her about the drawings the girl had scribbled at school: the saturated cucumbers. The government was coming to take the children away, all but the tallest.

Perhaps this is why a new president was not elected in George's body.

She had become voiceless.

She died on the operating table; she had swallowed her tongue.

The water began to boil up a storm. David took the pot and ran out the back door and filled the washbasin. It would skin him had he put his head in there right now. So he ran back to the house and gathered some cold water to add to it, before he opened his mouth and waited for the warm water to drown the cavity.

He could feel the tobacco juice going down. It had begun to taste like whiskey to him. He was growing dizzy, but it was all right. The pain was melting. The water was going inside his eardrum. Thank God he could hear the sound of healing. The world is not the same underwater.

He lifted his head up; the tobacco had begun to burn. He opened his eyes a little, and there was the ex-con standing over him. "Pass me some'n," he said. "Can't you see that I'm blind?"

David closed his eyes again. The ex-con had given him something; it felt like hide. Get away from me, David thought. I'm blind.

He fell back on the earth; with each attempt to open his lids, the sun seemed unbearable. He waited for the burning to stop. He touched the fabric in his hands. What was it? He couldn't think for the life of him what it was, until the burning began to wind down: it *was* hide—the hide of the rabbit whose skull he had crushed, dry now.

He would have killed the ex-con had he been able to see him clearly. But what man could get his house fenced for free, especially when he knew what barbwire could do to the human hand? Indeed, David Harris had built his own house with his mind. But barbwire drew blood and David Harris didn't have any more blood to lose; night after night, he was swallowing atomic pieces of the cavity. Hard enamel loosening up like particles of dust in his kidneys.

He stared at the ex-con from the ground; he was far away now, sliding the gloves back on his thick fingers, testing them. He saw his lips move and could not make out what he was saying. He wished the ex-con had broken his syllables down. Or that a whisper of wind had floated across his face and brought the syllables to him.

He sat up and looked at his clothes; he was soaked. He did not move for a while. He looked at the rabbit hide beside him; the mask facedown in a puddle of water. What was it supposed to do to him? Change him, perhaps. If there was anything to think about, he did not know what it was.

The words were there now on Logic's belly:
I will see.

chapter
thirty-one

David Harris knew how the sound of bone and muscle shivered when disturbed: he had imagined it, beneath the skin, turning slowly—like a metal chain coming down from a triangular house.

Too was a melting ice cube.

Her body loose, floating now.

chapter
thirty-two

It was Saturday.

Logic stood behind the tallest, eating berries. He made her put something in her stomach. They had somewhere to be. He was taking her to the other side, into the heart of Valsin County, Mississippi, with long cars and medium-sized buildings and the pharmacy and women who baked loaves of bread and carried them around in cloth. And the people—the people were made of real-life things: their feet trampling on the earth like music, the boys swinging newspapers and shit like that.

Everyone was made in America.

He was so excited to be able to take Logic; she had never been farther than that oak tree and the Missis' place and the operating room. He didn't even ask her about the blue purse. He had been up all night thinking about the route he would take past the pond. He went to sleep with the Italian philosopher's book on his chest to keep his heart from beating so very quickly.

The berries had not made any ground in Logic's stomach. She had eaten two handfuls. They were half sweet. Half sour. Like kiwi going down. "I done finished 'em," she said.

"Well," said the tallest, "let's go!"

It was early morning and Logic had left her mother behind. Too was turning flour over on a flat surface. And although the old woman was on the front porch humming, Too had not sent one flower across the road in memory of George.

Logic could see the clearings where the tallest had cut his way through. She was, indeed, on his side of Mississippi. There was a crowd of birds in the branches: heads turned, the white sky behind them, trembling.

Religion: there was none. Death: she did not feel it. Love: yes, love is what she felt. It moved around in her ribs for a short while, and then she heard it stop, as if suddenly taking a nap. Her spirit opened up, harmless.

The tallest came to a halt. "Hol' up a minute," he said. "Lemme catch my breath."

Logic was barely holding on; her stomach was hurting. But she never told him. She wanted to go to the outside.

Catching his breath was short-lived. The tallest took Logic by the hand again, and she could hear the cars on the concrete, the blowing of horns, and the newspaper boy yelling about the economy. And the women: they were walking on high-heeled shoes, like the tallest, and laughing and screaming at their children to stay close to them. She couldn't help but think they smelled like cotton candy.

When they made it to the edge of town, the tallest told her to hush. "All right," she said.

He knelt down in front of the road and took off his blue high-heeled shoes. He was barefoot now. He turned around and looked at Logic. "Act like you been to the other side your whole life," he said. "You hear me?"

"I hear," said Logic.

logic

He waited for a man in a three-piece suit to pass by and pulled Logic out of the woods.

They were now on the other side.

The tallest stopped in front of a window; there was a man holding a magazine up to his face with disgust, a woman in uniform. His stomach was pushed out and he had drunk a whole bottle of Coca-Cola, the empty glass beside him. The man's face was pink, the dark freckles like a comet in the middle of his forehead. The tallest stood there, Logic behind him, until the man recognized them in the window and shooed them away.

Logic was asking herself what the hand-sized machines were. It was the first time she had seen a pair of clippers. But there, down the road a piece, she saw a large sign, up high, above the others where the lady in the yellow hat disappeared, the lady who sold insurance to the dead.

But that was later.

For now, she watched a black man, painted white, standing on a crate, frozen. His nose was red; he had taken a bouncing ball and carved out the fat. The white folks threw money at him as he pulled on his suspenders and bowed. The tallest took her up close. She wanted to see what he was made of. She touched him; he was made of flesh, all right.

The tallest looked at her. "He ain't nothin' to crow after," said the tallest.

"How come?" asked Logic.

"'Cause he a nigger," he said. "Just like us."

Logic pulled away from him. "I ain't no nigger."

"You are on the other side," said the tallest. "Now, come on!"

They approached a woman carrying a sign: JESUS IS COMING BACK! ARE YOU SAVED?

Logic looked at the tallest. "What saved mean?"

"It mean the world ain't in you no more," he said.

The woman was redheaded. Her hair was not made of stomped wine but crimson. One of her legs was wooden and her eyes were sharp. She didn't even feel it when the newspaper boy threw a paper airplane at her chest. But Logic she felt, for Logic poked her in the stomach when she passed by. Logic turned around. The woman was looking up now.

"Jesus is coming back!" she yelled. "Are you saved?"

The newspaper boy had stopped in front of the soda-pop store. "Gimme a Coca-Cola!" he shouted. A black man, thin as a pair of shoelaces, came out from the booth and spanked him.

He was the man in the beginning.

"What I tell you 'bout that hollerin' 'n' so forth?" he asked.

The newspaper boy started to rub his eyes.

The man as thin as a pair of shoelaces spanked him again. "This the las' time I tell you 'bout that sassin'," he said. "Your mama don't work for Coca-Cola. You hear?"

The little boy nodded, as a white woman walked up behind him. "He givin' you problems, Mister Bear?" she asked the man as thin as a pair of shoelaces.

"Not no more," he said.

She put her hands on the little boy's shoulders. "You do what Mister Bear tells you, son," she said, before looking back up. "I got one I need you to straighten out, Mister Bear. He's got a snake on his tongue these days."

"Bring 'im right on to me," he replied. "These chaps ain't gone wurr me to death. Lawd knows I ain't got no insurance."

"I hear you, Mister Bear," said the white woman. "I'll bring him right on by the reckon."

"Yes, ma'am," said the man. "I'll straighten 'im out for you."

The tallest and Logic were standing next to a metal column across the road, cool on their faces. Logic had never seen a black man spank a white child. He seemed to be the Bear of all the white children. She could hear the clothespins in the spokes of the bicycle tires behind her, the children on the alabaster handlebars yelling out to the Bear. "I'm headin' home to my mama right now, Mister Bear," they'd say. "And I ain't been in no kind o' trouble! Ask her yourself!"

"All right," said Mister Bear, "I see to it."

He went back behind the wooden booth. The sign above him read: SIRVIN ALL KINDS OF JESUSES EN BEARLAND.

The newspaper boy had run off by now. Logic could hear him screaming around the corner of the buildings, as if he were looking for a titty to suck. She laughed. The tallest grabbed her hand; he had seen a water fountain just ahead.

Logic was confused. They had passed many water fountains along the way, even back where the man in the three-piece suit passed, before they had come out of the woods.

"You thirsty?" said the tallest.

"Uh-huh," she answered.

The tallest put his foot on the water petal and waited for the water to rise. "Go 'head," he said. "You prob'ly got me beat on thirst. But don't take too long. And don't talk whiles you drinkin' 'fore that stuff go down your windpipe."

"All right," she said, cooling her lips in the water.

"Put some on your face too," said the tallest.

She took up all the water she could in her dehydrated body. The tallest went next and drank till his belly stuck out. "If you ever come to town by yourself," he said. "Don't drink out of the Ws. Drink out of the Cs. Got it?"

"Uh-huh," said Logic.

"Where you wanna go to now?" he asked.

Logic pointed to the large sign she had seen far back.

"I ain't got no money for insurance, Logic," he said. "What you wanna go over there for?"

She shrugged her shoulders.

"Well," he said, "you go. You can stand right outside and look through the glass—like we did at the hair shop."

She nodded.

"And don't go stirrin' up the white folks. You hear?"

By then she was running toward the window where she had seen the insurance lady. It was not so much that she wanted to speak to her as it was that she had found a familiar person in an unfamiliar world.

She turned around and looked for the tallest between the crowd of people. Finally, she saw him standing back up at the water fountain, barefoot, his face hidden. She saw some white women standing in front of the store. Their fingers were white-gloved, as they patted their chests in the heat.

"Where you headed, Tilda?" said one of the white women.

"To the factory," said Tilda. "My maid's turnin' forty when the sun goes down. I wanted to get her a nice piece o' fabric 'fore I go home."

"Fabric?" replied the other white woman. "For your maid?"

Tilda was paying her no mind. She was digging in her purse, where Logic noticed a small red book with gold lining. "Yes," she said, "for my maid."

The other white woman tapped her on the shoulder and quickly began to walk away. Logic could hear her talking about the fabric and the nigger maid between a herd of women. Tilda was not concerned. She knelt beneath the sign; she was searching for a dime that had rolled out of the confines of her purse.

Logic picked it up.

A girl ran past her and into the insurance place, singing.

"Here you go, miss," said Logic, although the tallest was yelling for her to mind her own business.

The white woman looked up at her and smiled. "You just as cute as the baby Jesus," she said. "Since you were so kind as to pick that up off the ground, I reckon I'll let you keep it."

Logic nodded and before the woman turned around, she could not help but ask, "'Scuse me, miss," she said, pointing upward. "What that sign say?"

The white woman put out her white-gloved hand and touched her on the cheek. "Heaven," she said, before disappearing through the crowd.

Logic's eyes were loose with amazement. She stood in front of the window where the insurance lady was sitting at an oak-wood desk; her back was straight like the base of a pyramid, and there, sitting across from her, was the Missis, a pale handkerchief up to her face, supporting the bay of tears streaming from her pituitary gland.

The girl stood beside her, singing about telling. And the Missis reached into her purse and gave her a dime. The girl did not go away. She pinched her.

The tallest grabbed Logic by the arm. "I tol' you to stay to your own business, didn't I?" He was clearly upset. "Now we got to leave the other side and head for home." He was not running but strutting now. "Shoot!"

But Logic was ready to leave the other side. Although it was packed with cars and newspaper boys and Mister Bears and Miss Tildas, there was a loneliness in the world. At least, she could always talk to Celesta . . . whose birthday was coming up soon.

chapter
thirty-three

It was morning time.

The old woman and curtis were sitting on the front porch. The baby was asleep on her lap. She began to sing aloud. curtis repeated every word:

> *Trouble in my way*
> *Trouble in my way*
> *Gotta cry sometimes*
> *Gotta cry sometimes*

She paused for a moment, humming.

> *I know that Jesus,*
> *Jesus, He will fix it*
> *I know that Jesus,*
> *Jesus, He will fix it*

A hand in the heat . . .

> *Afterwhile.*

No one had told curtis where his mother had gone. While George was alive, she would rock him to sleep across her legs—even when waiting for the man-made-of-paper to show up, or other men—until he fell asleep. He'd wake up for a moment. And with her face against the pillows, she would put his hand on her chest. He would fall asleep to the rhythm of her beating heart.

Of course, she was aware of how he slept. She could hear him moaning when she was in the beds of men, listening to them breathe as they cloaked the air in her lungs. One night, during a visit from the man-made-of-paper, she caught a flying insect in her hand. It moved, the torso vibrating. The wings active. And the following night, the darkness around her, she waited for curtis to fall asleep; then peeled the casing back from the pillow and taped the insect down.

So that when he reached for her, he could still hear the pounding of her heart.

He stood behind the old woman. Although he had been at the burial, he was too young to be concerned with reactions. He had seen the old woman break down in front of him. But why? Everything in his life was a shadow. The old woman was a dinosaur. The tallest, his brother, was an amphibian. The girl, nothing. The houses around him, boxes and boxes of unhappiness. He did know this much: pain came in squares. If you touched the corners of it, you would find the sharpness of knives.

Perhaps the old woman felt the government was coming.

She had been in George's room, emptying her things out on the bed. She knew what she wanted the children to have on their skin: the love of George. She put their clothes and things on the bed and powdered them down. A child is worthless without the scent of his mother. She had written a note and stuffed it into the polyester lining of the suitcase—she covered her hands when she wrote it—and put a picture of George in there: she was on her stomach laughing, her feet bare, her head laid across a red blanket.

Too had grown tired of looking through the kitchen window. She was thinking of Logic now. She had gone to her room the night before to put the pajamas on a hard surface; she had seen Logic lying on her back, the candle at play on the windowsill, and noticed the small pouch rising underneath the covers. Perhaps it had always been there. Perhaps she was pygmified like the babies in the yellow magazines. She asked nothing of Logic, for there was nothing, even in her cold heart, that kept her safe.

She vowed never to look at Logic again.

Not only with her eyes, but to pretend, almost as if cruelty was all she had left, that she was dead. She had been buried with the prostitute underneath the oak tree. She did not care if she carried iron or what she was doing with it. Or wool. Or that her stomach was rising.

Logic was dead.

When this thought came over her, she felt a shift in the temperature around her. She had never been afraid of being alone in the house. She sat still. Things moved in silence, didn't they? she thought. A pause. Silence again and the breaking of it by the ex-con; he was running a herd of Brahma out of the adjacent field.

Too patted her chest and sighed. She would not admit that she was still afraid. David was off at the woodyard. Maybe it was his pattern of footsteps in the house that formed a ghost around her. Surely, it could have been. Or the chain ticking against the rooftop. She had begged him to get rid of it; he had gotten a large metal hook from the woodyard and connected it to the tail end of the chain. He wouldn't dare.

Now she could hear the child she had let go of. She was on the porch clinging to something. She could always tell when Logic clung to something. Her feet were pressed against the boards of the man-built house; the fabric of her toes was loud. And her arms were stretched out, the fingers on the columns tied together by the force of her hands to grab hold.

Logic could hear her too. Even in the silence of the house, she knew her mother was sitting still at the kitchen table, breathing as though she were alone in the world. Logic had been over to the Missis', stapling her wings together. She had wrapped the wool perfectly around the iron hangers; all she had left was the tail end of the insect to mold. The Missis told her to sit up straight and pulled the ribs of the iron hangers together so the wings could sprout out. She had given Logic a piece of red velvet to tie around her neck, to hold up the wings. It was perfect, Logic thought. Everything. Everything was perfect.

The tallest had not come outside since Logic had made it home. But she saw the bridge of his arm rise occasionally from his bedroom window; when he felt what he could not afford, he pulled it back. The old woman was sitting out on the porch swatting flies, curtis lying on her lap, arms hanging.

Everyone heard the rocks moving: a car on the road. Even Too, with the activity of silence around her, knew that someone was coming to stir up the house across the road.

It was the goverment.

The old woman woke curtis up. She began to shake him out of his sleep. He tried to wrap his arms around her neck. He simply wanted to dream.

"You got somewhere to be," she said, rousing him again. "You hear?"

Instantly, his eyes opened.

"Remember what we talked about?"

He wiped his eyes. "Yes'm."

"All right," said the old woman. "You be a big boy now."

He would have said yes'm had he agreed. But he could not. Her words had come out in squares. He began to cry loudly. She had frightened him.

She did not need to talk to the girl. The girl was fully dressed, her hands behind her back clenching paper. There she was on the steps of the wooden house, waiting for the government to take her away.

"Stay here," whispered the old woman. curtis could not loosen the danger around him.

By then, the car had pulled up. The lady sitting behind the wheel was glaring out ahead of her. Her face was the color of a dying magnolia, her hair white. It seemed as if nothing in her life had ever crumbled. She had come straight out of a factory.

The old woman was holding the baby now. She looked down at the brown face, the hands trembling. Then she looked out at the lady who stood at the base of the steps, holding the energy in the girl's hand.

"Keep 'em wit' they own kind," she said. "Don't go messin' 'em up on the inside." She paused. "You hear?"

The lady nodded.

By now, the girl was in the front seat of the car, the heat going down her stomach. curtis had not yet come out. The old woman called for him and he came running. "I want you to get in that car wit' this here lady and don't look back," she said. "Find you some'n God made and love on it. But don't you look back on Valsin County."

The old woman never really looked at curtis. Or the girl. None of them, not even the baby, was hers to keep.

chapter
thirty-four

It had begun to rain.

Logic was in her room. She was not lying flat or creating an atmosphere of laughter. She was in the mirror with her arms beside her. Had she something to cling to her ribs besides the symmetry of bones themselves, she would have known better than to pretend. She was in a white cloud of fragility. She had heard the answer in the blowing out of the candle: Fly.

She was becoming a part of something rapid.

It was not meant to be controlled.

The wings hung on the wall. She wished she could have eaten them. Like the feeling, she had dreamed of swallowing an idea. It was packed down inside of her, molecular. White. She was sitting on a curb, as if waiting for the idea to settle down and let her catch it. But it traveled through her; its noise had even awakened the sun, the yellow rim of its circle burning.

Nothing could stop the idea.

It was habit that saved her. Even in her dreams, she could feel the leech crawling on her head. And when she swallowed, she had, by accident, digested the idea; the white cloud rose within her and pushed her stomach out. But habit was only good for sleeping.

The world is different upon waking up.

Celesta was in the bed. Logic had begun to talk to her. She was starving too.

David was on his way home from the woodyard. The rain had begun to vibrate in the trees; he could hear it falling on the roof of his house. He had planned it this way, hoped that when the water pelted the tin roof that it would disturb Too, anyone. He hated the conversation of marriage, even before he had begun to keep quiet. There was always the silence of discomfort—the long two-edged breath between him and Too, him and the rest of the world. He needed division.

He almost thought he heard someone behind him. He put his hand on his hips. He hoped he had brought his pistol. But he had not. He had grown careless these days. There was an ax sitting up inside of him, the blade struck on a cord of something useful. Or what had been.

Maybe it was the ex-con, he thought.

He wanted it to be. He had seen him at the woodyard walking through a dark cloud. Not the collection of dust in the air but the energy of a tangible wire, a metal line of hopelessness following him around. Unraveling in smoke. He was a burning ice cube.

David had not yet forgotten how he looked at him. He had hoped that perhaps once, while toting the logs through the woodyard, the ex-con would become pinned beneath the weight of the wood some-how, hoped that the ex-con would come calling on him, the way he had, himself, waited on the tobacco to stop burning. So he could take the life right out of his foot and reach down, stop light.

But it never happened.

David could see Too in the window of the house. There was no lightning or thunder. He had prayed for it. He wished it were the

Missis' bed she was sleeping in tonight. He had begun to hate the sound of her breathing.

When he opened the door, her face was turned toward the stove. Her arms were in the pockets of her apron, her spine forward. Part of him wanted to touch her, to see if she was made of blood. He looked down at her feet. Perhaps she had stepped into a small pool of water, her feet bound to the stove by an exposed current of electricity. But she had not. He felt the warmth of her shoulders, the cartilage going to sleep. And turned away.

Logic heard him coming. She closed her eyes, Celesta's face frozen in the darkness. She had balanced the air in her room, knew when it was violated. The footsteps grew closer.

David was standing over her.

Too had never known him to go in her room after the light was out. She moved from where she was and picked up the porcelain dishes stacked high on the table. They were not hers. They belonged to the Missis and she had brought them home to clean. This was the noise that she had needed, desired at that moment. Because there, past the operating room, was the sound of David's shoes stirring.

But they only stirred to leave the room.

Because Logic had begun to pray.

The moon, turned sun, was bearing down on the ex-con as he stretched the last row of barbwire through the first two poles of his work. He felt most comfortable alone. The laughter had gotten to him at the woodyard. The men had Os in their mouths. They had simple things to laugh about. If they had been born with any seriousness in them, they had killed it.

In a few days, his work would be done. What was he to do? The government had him tied down to Valsin County. He had already given them an address. He regretted it now.

He looked out into the field. Everything dyed green. Everything in spears, growing. He did not have an ax inside of him, but he was out of place in the natural world. And although The Principle had tormented him, he belonged there in his cell on the block. He had not been able to sleep without the noises spilling out from the stone jungle: the guards shouting above him, from the top level of the prison, for the feathers to go to bed. He had become used to confinement, left to imagine what the green looked like, smelled like on the outside.

He belonged in concrete.

He himself was a cavity. He was a dark space and could feel the weight of a monster sitting on the mouth of the cave. His hands open. There, beating in his chest, was a need to make something move.

What was he to do when the barbwire had run out? He had asked himself if he'd find more fences to put up. And keep going, until all the fences in Valsin County were barbwired. He looked at his hands, the mahogany lines under the skin. They had been torn apart.

This was where he lived, in the mahogany, where the blood ran through him, saving him from nothing. He saw Logic's belly in the open window of her bedroom. She was swollen on the inside, her fingers on the windowsill, spreading.

The circular bone in her wrist was dead. She turned away, her fingers disappearing. He could hear her talking to Celesta. She was no jiver like the boys in prison, he thought. Her voice was flat. It could have reached a continent of running animals had she allowed it to get away.

He stood there awhile, wondering what his own daughter sounded like now. He had seen her in his dreams, in the shape of a question mark.

Had the ex-con been able to have more children, he would have dreamed less of them. The prison had sterilized him. Although the doctor told him that there was no way a man could feel his sterility leaving him, the ex-con disagreed. He did feel it. He felt it out on the yard, while bench-pressing the iron dumbbells. It traveled through his abdomen—where his ovaries would have lived, had he been born a woman—to the cord in his penis and into the air. He knew that his semen was on the ground now, for it had not known how to fly.

Because the condition of looking down was in his bones.

There, in the window, was a child pushed out from the inside. She herself was made of concrete. He had seen her running toward the oak tree, as if she didn't care about falling on her belly. He had never seen her touch it, not in all the days that he had worked there behind the house. She carried on like this at all times; she must have thought that she was a belly surgeon. Made to fix her stomach had she broken it on the ground, he thought.

He saw her fingers reappear on the edge of the windowsill. They were no longer spreading but solid. She had said something and meant it. No nervousness there in her thin body. Just the sound of Celesta falling off the side of the bed, because she did not have the vertebrae to sit up straight.

chapter
thirty-five

David had not yet shaken the sleep off of him. He was lying in bed, thinking of the night the man had pulled a gun on him. He had been sitting at a jook joint with a half-filled glass of whiskey. He had not yet begun to carry guns. He had not yet felt danger growing around him. The man sat at a table across from him. He could not remember the contours of his face or the manner in which he breathed under a red light. But he had gotten into an argument with him—something about foreigners—the man yelled that we are all foreigners living in our foreign selves. The argument had only lasted a matter of minutes when their voices began to settle down.

David had told himself he would forget it, that the man was some drunken fool. A mechanism. He sat there, the whiskey circulating. And as the hours passed, he looked around for the time. But it could not be found. He had memorized the last three numbers on the back of the bottle before him: 314. It was what a man did out of boredom in Mississippi. He concentrated on the immobility of a solid object and played with the paralyzed thing in his head.

He concentrated on sanity.

Then there was the sound of lead: one click, a pistol. The hairs rose on the back on his neck. His heart began to drown. Because he knew, everyone knew, that it was the sound of the man holding a gun to the back of his head.

"Next time, nigger," said the man, "you'll know when danger comes." The man knelt down to him; David had forgotten the numbers, the paralyzation of things in threes: "'Cause you loaded the gun."

When he felt security around him again, he turned around.

The man was gone.

And from that moment on, he had blocked the encounter out of his head. He went to Pyke County and bought his own lead and toted it around until he felt safe again. He was a man. And no one would ever pull a gun on him again. Ever.

Too was getting ready to bring a baby into the world. She was naked. He looked at her imperfect body, the dark line going up her stomach. Her flat breasts. Between her legs was a patch, a nest growing. He wanted to cut it out and set it on the limb of a tall tree. This was her only worth to him; the rest of her was acidic.

"I'm headin' out," she said. "Be back attawhile to snap the beans."

He turned over in the bed. He imagined the green in her hands. She was unworthy of responsibility, he thought. He had, himself, been in her hands. Because he needed strength.

And she was made of concrete.

"You hear me?" she said. "I'm goin' to pull a baby out."

He moaned. "I heard you."

It came out this way, the rest of his words gasoline.

"I said I'll be back to snap the beans," said Too.

Beans. They were like babies in her hands, careless naïveté. Green.

logic

He drove her away with a flip of his hand.

He was a line of barbwire, now.

The heat was suffocating.

The old woman and the Missis were both traveling to the porches of their houses. Their arms had come down in the same degree. Down from the brow. Then away, next to the hip.

The Missis had stopped eating entirely. It would have taken more than the tallest to fill her house with activity. She was slipping away from her own journey, if she knew why she felt this way. A woman needs to know what she is made of; even she is aroused by an idea, a climax of feeling.

She did not even find God in the trees, the sun, or the ringing of the church bells anymore. The dimes, out of which she was to pay Logic, were stretched out on the kitchen table. One for every day of the week. Because she knew that death comes from living in the sharpness of momentary disasters: when the red begins to shout.

Now Logic and the tallest were walking toward her. She had heard him swinging from the tree, his hips on the oak, his body upside down. The sound of his voice collapsing at the palate; the wilting larynx.

The tallest lay down on the porch. He was out of breath.

"You thirsty?" asked the Missis.

He sat up on his elbows, his back on the boards. "Yeah," he said, "I'm thirsty."

Logic had disappeared into the house.

"I thought you'd never come," said the Missis.

There was a cloud of weariness running in the tallest's chest. Now he could see the face of the woman he had saved. He looked at her, the freckles of gravity on her skin. There was nothing genuine about her, not even gravity. Or her wine-colored hair. He could not let her get close to him, could not believe that this was the woman he had saved.

He looked away from her, as if she were made of history.

Logic ran back out on the porch and handed the tallest a glass of water and disappeared again. He set the water down beside him. The cloud of weariness within him had vanished.

"What's wrong wit'chu, white woman?" he asked.

"Nothing," she said.

"Yeah," said the tallest. "You climbing a mountain."

The Missis looked at him; the elephant in his forehead had gone to sleep.

The tallest lay back on the porch, his arms out. "You got Jesus?"

"Somewhere, I s'pose."

The tallest shook his head. "What you think?" he said, looking back at the lamb on the stained-glass door of her house. "You think the government done run off with 'im?"

The Missis smiled a little, her lips ajar. "No."

The tallest jumped up and grabbed her chin; she let him. "You talk like you got the Abe Lincolns," he said, counting the freckles going up the side of her cheek.

Of course he knew it, was not polite about it.

The white woman was dead.

"Perhaps," said the Missis.

So silent was the scent of the tallest that it hung there like the cloud it was, as it had in her bedroom, and went to sleep.

"You a crazy ol' white woman," said the tallest, releasing her face to the air. "You done caught the Abe Lincolns. Now you gotta find yourself a place in the sky."

"Or down under," she said.

"Go'lee," said the tallest. "You talk like you ain't 'fraid o' nothing. But I bet you are. I bet you are 'fraid o' something."

She shrugged her shoulders.

"What you got down off in you?" asked the tallest, circling her, his bare feet rotating.

"Sadness," she said.

The tallest laughed and stepped away from the porch for a moment, looking up at the glass windows of her bedroom. "All right to be sad, white woman. Jesus was sad. But He damn sure wadn't depressed."

She was a silent river.

The tallest heard the bells ring at the roof of the house. "I ain't comin' back over here no more," he said. "You ain't come down off the mountain yet. And I got shoes to stuff."

He had put tissue paper in the tips of his mother's blue high-heeled shoes, and he would do this until his feet were tucked away in there perfectly.

Logic was coming.

The tallest took the Missis' face in his hands again. "There's a place folks go to burn," he said. "And if I catch you down there, you gettin an ass-whoopin'."

Logic opened the stained-glass door and began to run away from the Missis' house, stuffing the dime in her pocket with one hand. Crushed velvet was in the other; she had the tail to her wings now.

The tallest saw her disappear through the trees. He looked back at the Missis and touched her wine-colored hair, as if she had been plastic, before running off past the oak tree, yelling for Logic to wait for him.

* * *

Leave the boy alone.

She had tricked him, lying there like that, pale sugar in the grass, and expecting to be saved. Had he done what he really wanted, he would have pushed her right on out of that chair and pointed to the grave, told her to reach her foot out to where his mother was and tell her right to her face, right there where the bones were: No, you are not brave.

This is brave.

chapter
thirty-six

Logic had begun stitching the velvet tail to the ribs of the wings. She wanted it there in the center. Tomorrow was Celesta's birthday. She had laid her on the dresser sideways, her hands thrown behind her back. Eyes gone.

The picture of the tallest's pituitary gland was still taped to the mirror. She punctured the spine of the tail with the needle and walked over to it. She had never truly looked at the tiny blue mark at the tail end of the winding sphere, the orange. She put her hand over it and thought about the day she had gone to the other side, the berries in her stomach, the sudden feeling of the butterflies no longer floating.

Almost instantly, as does a girl when her pores are open for the first time, she knew that there were no floating insects in her belly.

The butterflies were seamen, the name she had seen on one of the Missis' magazines, above the kitchen window, where the woman was dressed in uniform, her lips parted. This is how she spelled the passage of arrows traveling up from her father's penis to her open vagina.

Seamen.

She knew, for the first time, that the baby in her stomach had died.

The last and only thing that had gone into its mouth was the blue liquid of berries.

Her baby was dead.

Because she could not open her mouth and eat the food of the world.

She lay back on her bed and touched her vagina, the abdomen as still and useless as a pituitary gland in the wrong place. She would not go to the tallest and ask him to pull the weight out of her swollen body or take out the tools of surgery to find out if the head or feet was to come out first. She was in another place. She was as cold as her own mother now. She sat up on the edge of the bed and walked into the operating room. Her fingers were crawling on the metal now. She, too, had been the slaughtered. She hoped that Jesus would walk through the doors of this house, after she had left the world, and wake the hell out of the living. Wake them up from their sleeps, her mother while having the Johnsons and David while dreaming of the man.

She began to cry.

Her mind was leaving her. She did not hear the pulling of the barbwire in the backyard by the ex-con. Or the old woman across the road beating the tallest for the eye shadow on the bridge of his lids. She heard nothing.

She wished she had not let the lightning bugs go. She needed them to live in the darkness of her body, to sanitize her. She needed living light. She realized, more than anything else, that she was dead.

She did not say her prayers that night, the prayers she had discovered on a distant grave. Instead, she worked endlessly on the velvet tail, stitching it perfectly to the center of the wings. She was ready to fly.

chapter
thirty-seven

He was that He is.

chapter
thirty-eight

It was July 22.

And Celesta was ready to eat.

Too was at the Missis', rearranging the cups and saucers to match the linoleum. She had not understood what had gotten into the Missis. The woman had not come downstairs all morning; she had begun to speak of nonliving things.

A white helicopter was flying above Valsin County. The propellers ricocheted through the clouds as Too stood there alone, the veins in her wrists pulsating rapidly.

She called for the Missis and noticed, there on the kitchen table, enough dimes to last Logic the rest of her life. Perhaps, she thought, the Missis had heard about Logic giving her money away for George's funeral and wanted to give it back to her.

This was the end of her imagination.

She listened, but she never heard—not even the church bells chiming from the rooftop at dusk or the whisper of David's hand circling the wall of their bedroom at night, the same wall Logic had circled, night after night, to silence him.

The helicopter was gone. She could see the separation of clouds it had left behind. It was flying over another county now. Floating.

A porcelain plate was in her hands warning of a hairline fracture; the Missis had been holding it in the darkness when it almost fell to the floor. Her reflection startled her; she thought she had seen a vowel.

Too called for the Missis again. She assured herself it was the splitting headache that had kept her in bed. She had been complaining of a throbbing migraine; she even felt it in her eardrums, repeating itself in a pattern of loose vocabulary. Her head was running wild.

Too eventually stopped calling and pressed her fingers on her ribs. She thought she had cracked a bone from the inside. Maybe it was troubling an organ, rousing it out of a deep sleep.

She sat down at the table, the porcelain plate centered on the bed of dimes around her. The Johnsons were wearing her out. She could not help but be alive. She had felt the man inside her abdomen, playing his guitar on the side of a wooden house. His strings, the music of her body like a dime box with the chimes of a dancing ballerina. Her ovaries, absent the scent of babies, the lead of his instrument.

David Harris was thinking of no one. His mind was free of all things. He looked out at the men in the woodyard. They had never really meant anything to him. He had never carried them home with him or invented a line for them in his prayers. The ex-con no longer counted. In his mind, he had killed him.

His tooth had completely healed. The tobacco had sunken down into the root and filled the tracks of his gums. He did not need to go to the other side to be cured. He had swallowed light; it was still buried in his body. He himself thought he had sensed it swimming through a pool of water in his loins. There was nothing catastrophic about David Harris.

Not now.

logic

* * *

No one ever knew what time it was in Valsin County, Mississippi. Perhaps they should have.

The sun was turning the corner; dusk was near.

David Harris was walking past the oak tree when he stopped for a moment. He looked at George's grave and wondered how deep she was in the ground. He imagined the experiments of the dead, the doctors tapping on the brain to make the mouth open. They could have used her, he thought.

He heard someone above him, the whistling noise of the boy he had called many times, in his head, a faggot. It was the tallest, staring down on him.

"What you want wit' my mama?" said the tallest.

David laughed. He knew his laughter was a sharp blade. "Boy," he said, "you wish you had the answer to me, don't you?"

The tallest jumped down from the tree. "Why you reckon?" he said. "'Cause I asked you for some sugar?"

David Harris stopped laughing. The nerve of the faggot to fuck with him. He could still smell the blood of the rabbit in his clothes, the killing he did not regret because he did not know how to.

He wanted to slap the tallest across his face. Instead, he turned away, saying, "You don't have the answer to me. Nobody got the answer to me. Not even the man."

As he walked away, the tallest lay beside his mother's grave, the elephant in his forehead rising. His life had come to separation. He had grown used to it now. If he had gotten over losing her, everyone else was perishable.

The old woman sat on the porch across the road, watching David Harris pause in front of his house. Her eyes were on a high branch; there was a cloud in her face. Had she touched the warm blood there, it would have floated clean out of her, into the world, growing dark now.

David Harris turned and looked at her. She was a match waiting to burn. And he had better things to do than save lives. He stiffened his shoulders at the door's opening, walked toward the faucet with one hand on his gut, and sighed deeply before putting the gun in the kitchen window.

His feet were covered in mud.

He grew silent.

The dime box began to chime. The scent of the operating room had deadened the air in the house. It was a mixture of him and her, Man and Woman.

Celesta was sitting at the kitchen table; her mouth was stapled again.

Dinner was prepared. Logic had spent the day boiling rabbit. She set it on one of the porcelain plates of the Missis, abandoned by Too. The skull was still attached to the neck, the eyes open. She had skinned it herself, on the tree; she had watched David. Watched him do everything. And there, beside it, was the paring knife she had used to carve the words on her belly, the carving of the letters filled with red ink.

David Harris did not know what to do. He could have used the blade of his laughter again, but he had begun to silently memorize something, as he had the numbers on the bottle of whiskey: 314.

He sat down at the kitchen table, across from Celesta.

Maybe, he thought, Logic had forgiven him. It had been awhile since he had taken her to the operating room and lifted her clothes. And he had prayed to God in her name, prayed that her stomach would go down or that she would come into natural disaster. Or better yet, forgiveness.

This is what it was.

She was forgiving him.

He looked at Celesta. Her eyes were set back in the bone. They had been stitched in with fishing twine. Her shirt was pulled up to the belly. She could have been born of cartilage or bone now. She was alive.

David Harris picked up the paring knife and began to cut the meat before him. It was still a part of the ribs, the gutted intestines replaced with the scent of dust. He paused and looked over at the stove—where he had hoped that Too could have been electrocuted—and threw himself into laughter again. He was safe . . . until Logic walked into the kitchen, the wings of the lamb attached to her back at the waist.

"Logic," he said, "you got your daddy in you."

"I know," she said, her crumbling feet on the floor around him, walking softly to the window where the tallest was now pushing his face through the screen door of his house.

"This some good kill, Logic Harris," he said.

She touched her stomach and walked over to the stove where the water had been wiped clean. The ex-con was in the backyard tying up the last of the barbwire on the poles. His job was done at the Harrises', and he had grown tired of waiting for the train to come. He would rather go back to The Principle than be tied to Valsin County, Mississippi. If the government owned him now, they owned what was inside of him, even the tracks of a freedom train.

"Jesus," said David Harris.

Logic watched him take down the rabbit. The paring knife had been sharpened.

He had collided with gravity.

She then looked at Celesta, her body pinned to the wooden chair so that she would know what it was to sit up straight. There was no penis to validate her.

"I know how to spell heaven now," said Logic.

David Harris looked up from the rabbit, the paring knife in his hands. His body had a loose circuit in it, and it was about to ignite. "Girl," he said, "you can't spell heaven. You think you spell heaven by lookin' up."

Logic said nothing. She stood with her back to the stove. Night had come and she could hear the earth trembling. She wished her baby had trembled like this, at least one more time, so the taste of berries would not have been the only feeling it had left of the world.

David Harris thought about what she had said and pulled his laughter out again. "Heaven," he said. "You can't spell heaven." He thought of something worse to say, something destructive. He laid the paring knife down beside the porcelain plate. "'Cause you retarded."

Instantly, she thought of the tallest and what he had written down in the dust: *Blow their brains out.*

The loaded pistol was there in the window. It was all she had. No, it was not all she had, but it was what she wanted.

David Harris picked up the paring knife again. He had almost devoured the rabbit, down to the ribs, when the hairs on his head stood up. He knew the feeling of a gun at his back. "Logic," he whispered, "what you got in your hands?"

She was silent.

Now she could raise her hand to him.

The gun.

The gun was an action verb.

The red had caught up with the blue again and she saw the vein beating sideways at the edge of his mouth like the time he asked a man what phosphorus had to do with fire . . . and he breathed from within and lit a match.

"Logic," whispered David Haris, "what you got in your hands?"
Her hand was on the trigger. "Nothing," she said.

Too picked up the Missis' hand. She was in the porcelain bathtub, swollen from head to foot, her hair muddy. There, beside her,
a diary where she had laid her words down; it was turned to the page
of a loud, solitary word: MOLESTED. But by this time, David Harris
was lying facedown on the kitchen table, his brains blown out.

Because he had loaded the gun.

epilogue

After he heard the shot fired, the ex-con walked through the back door of David Harris's house, found Logic standing behind him, her wings bloody. And picked the gun up off the floor, disappearing.

Logic herself did not know the next moments of her own life. Somehow, she made it to the roof of her house, the metal chain around her shoulders, the blue purse that had slept under her bed for many nights in her hand. There, she had caught the wind of the earth. Up high where dead things go when buried. At least, she had prayed this in her dreams.

She stood at the edge of the rooftop. "In His will is my peace," she whispered.

And jumped.

David Harris would have wanted her dead, wanted her red to shout.

The tallest would have cried had he any crying left in him. Instead, he walked up to Logic's fallen hand and lifted the blue purse up off the ground. He was surprised the egg hadn't slipped right down Logic's leg, hanging there like that. He went to lift the dress, but the body was so obscure, so fascinating while dead, that he knew it impossible for the egg to wake.

And so it was that he had no more lives to save.

The faggot.

The sissy.

Call him what you want: no one would stop him from living. Not now.

Everyone heard it, at the present hour; the voice of the old woman was riveting:

Hope me.
Somebody hope me.

What power did she have to run across the road and take that child down from the rooftop? Perhaps she could have held one body, one child Logic's size, and brought it onto the porch and prayed over it, but the child carried a bird in that tiny body of hers.

And it was yet rotating.

The old woman's hand came down from her brow, as it had this time of evening, and when the tallest came walking toward her she reached out to grab him but felt the tapping of her father's spirit on the palm of her hand. This time, it was not the question, Will it hurt? but, Let him be.

Too Harris had heard it.

Yes, Too Harris, it was a gun you heard.

Her hands were still wet.

Something awaited her.

She must hurry.

She grabbed hold of the railing and stopped for a spell; it was so cold.

She began to run, could not run quickly enough.

She opened the door of the house and turned, without smiling, to the blade of grass that lay singularly on the floor. It seemed so important. She wanted to stay, to be this thing without urgency or routine, so she could lie there where it was and be impossible.

She had heard Logic calling her, heard her say it: *Mama.*

But it was only in her head.

For when she lifted Logic's dress, there lay the words on her round belly: *I will see you again in.* . . . The last word was an arrow, pointing upward.

But Logic.
Logic was not dead.
She could never be.

acknowledgments

To the alphabet.

In memory of Atreyu Frazier.

Ms. Barbara and Mr. Ed of East Laville Hall.

The man on I-35: in memory of your wife and children.

To Hilton Gray: I am grateful.

Special thanks to LSU, SLU, MCLA.

The city of New Orleans for its outstanding support.

The Salon Girls: Beverly House-Leonard, Karen Hutchison, Ossie Joseph, Gilda Lee, Yolanda Barra, Cassandra Peters, Joanetta Williams, and, of course, the moving spirit Ms. Joyce. To Lynn Hutchison and Shantal Hubbard.

For answering: Yavon D. Robinson, Susie Campbell, Armelle Kouton, Marta Bell of LSU, Jessie Elliott, Mary Gay Shipley for arriving in snow, her wonderful staff at TBIB, Veronica Holliday, Kathryn Mackenroth, wherever you are, Kevin Darouse, Jelani Foster, Shante Thompson, Bruce Alford, and Elaine Coney, Michelle Sutton-Williams.

To Grove/Atlantic for the second round.

Special thanks to the St. Albert Catholic Center and their staff for helping us (Armelle, John, Eugene Breslin, Ha, Juba, Mr. and

Mrs. Harvey Jones, the Daily Star, the city of Hammond, and other volunteers) ship clothes to the children of Africa.

To Carol Mackey of Black Expressions, Thumper, Marlive Harris of GRITS, AALBC, Gwendolyn Williams and The Readers of CA, Christena Coleman and Just Between Girlfriends, the Sistah Circle, Carole McAllister and the Hammond Group, RAWSISTAZ Reviewers, Book Remarks, the Black Library, Imani Book Club, Between Friends Literary Group, Sista Friendz, and all others for your outstanding support.

To Mrs. Linda Fortenberry and Mr. Hugh (for your incredible eye), Mrs. Kathleen James, and Mrs. Janis Smith of Washington Parish. Ms. Kathy for the yearbooks.

To A. Cimino: the butterfly is here, alive.